"What [barcode] **shriek**

She was awakened from her erotic dream to find herself being dragged from the bed and slung upside down fireman-style over Trevor's shoulder. She blinked furiously, trying to clear the cobwebs.

"What are you doing?" This demand was delivered to the very hard, very broad back of... Wait a minute. Her dream man wasn't real, was he? No, she reasoned, she must still be asleep after all. But with the well-muscled arm strapped across the backs of her thighs, she realized her predicament was definitely real.

The breath she'd planned to use to inform him of his mistake was oomphed out of her as he stepped off the porch and headed toward his car. She was outside—in her underwear. "Oh, my God! I don't have any clothes on!"

"I've got them. You can dress at the church. Save the excuses—" Trevor cut her off "—whatever they are."

Christy was dumped in the front seat of the car and was just winding up to deliver a blistering speech to this Neanderthal. But as she turned to confront him, the words died in her throat. He was the most gorgeous Neanderthal she'd ever laid eyes on....

Dear Reader,

I've enjoyed mistaken identity stories ever since
Hayley Mills appeared as twins in the Disney movie
The Parent Trap. Of course, now I've grown up a little,
and my fantasies have grown up along with me.When
my editor called and asked me to take part in THE
WRONG BED series, I thought here was the perfect
time to fulfill that particular fantasy!

I had the best time torturing my characters Trevor and
Christy during their initial meeting (though I don't let
the mistaken part go on for very long). But by then
they are irrevocably involved with each other. I hope
you enjoy watching what starts out as a mistake turn
into love.

Happy reading!

Donna Kauffman

Books by Donna Kauffman

HARLEQUIN TEMPTATION
828—WALK ON THE WILD SIDE
846—HEAT OF THE NIGHT

HARLEQUIN BLAZE
18—HER SECRET THRILL

CARRIED AWAY
Donna Kauffman

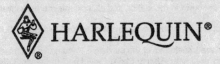

HARLEQUIN®

TORONTO • NEW YORK • LONDON
AMSTERDAM • PARIS • SYDNEY • HAMBURG
STOCKHOLM • ATHENS • TOKYO • MILAN • MADRID
PRAGUE • WARSAW • BUDAPEST • AUCKLAND

This book is dedicated to the guys at Crucible.
Thanks for making this world a little bit safer
for those in need.

ISBN 0-373-25974-3

CARRIED AWAY

Printed in U.S.A.

____Prologue____

"SHE'S NOT COMING. I knew it!"

Trevor McQuillen shifted uncomfortably. There was nothing more terrifying than being alone with an unhappy bride on her wedding day. Except perhaps a *crying* unhappy bride. When tears pooled in Kate's eyes, Trevor knew he had to take action. "Listen, maybe she just got caught up—"

"No, she's not here because someone told her Eric was going to be at the reception. She told me not to invite him and I swore I wouldn't, but I—I just had to do something!" Her bottom lip began to quaver. "I just wanted her to be happy. Like I am with Mike. Viv and Eric belong together and I thought once she was here, with all the sentimentality of the wedding—" She broke off on a gulp of air and a noisy sniff.

Okay, Trevor schooled himself, *don't panic*. Five minutes, that's all Mike had asked. Keep her company for five minutes until her dad arrived. Trevor had commanded sensitive covert operations in four different countries over the past five years. Surely he could handle one crying woman. Mike would never forgive him if he handed over a blubbering bride.

So he did what Lieutenant Commander Trevor McQuillen did best. He assessed the situation and took command of the operation. Kate wanted Vivian to be in her wedding party. If Trevor could fly halfway around the world to stand up for his best buddy, this Vivian could certainly get over herself and whatever problems she'd had with Eric to do the same for her best friend. "Do you know where she is?"

Kate was rubbing her nose with a wad of tissues, and his barked order made her jump. "Wha—? Where Viv is?"

Trevor clamped his jaw tight and willed the tic under his right eye to stop jumping. For once he was happy he was an only child. In a gentler tone, he said, "Yes, ma'am. If you'll direct me to where she is, I'll go and get her. Bring her here."

Kate was already shaking her head, but the way her watery blue eyes lit up with hope, Trevor knew he was going to do this, even if he had to personally put this Viv into her bridesmaid's dress and truss her into the back seat of his rental sedan.

"She's—she's probably at home. I got Tricia to call her, but she didn't pick up."

Trevor had no idea who Tricia was—probably one of the dozen or so bridesmaids presently dressing and chattering in the room above the alcove they were standing in. "But you think she's there?"

She hiccuped and nodded. "I don't know where

else she'd go." Fresh tears threatened as she gulped in a deep breath. "What was I thinking to play matchmaker on my wedding day?"

Trevor wondered the same thing, but time was of the essence here.

"I just thought it would be so romantic, you know?" She tried to smile as her breath hitched. "I know they still love each other. What better place to realize that than at a wedding?"

"But you believe she's at home now?" Trevor silently begged her to focus on the solution, not the problem. He'd been risking his life for too long making solutions happen despite people's refusal to focus. Apparently turning civilian wasn't going to end that job description. At least not yet. "How far away is it?"

"Five, maybe ten minutes tops."

He handed her his handkerchief when her tissue finally gave out, trying not to wince when she used it noisily. He shook his head when she offered it back to him and searched the alcove for something to write with. He took the wedding program from the pocket of his dress uniform and scooped up the little half pencil from a box filled with tithe envelopes. "Directions?"

Kate looked uncertain. "What if she—? I mean, I...don't want to—"

"This is your wedding day and you want her to be here to witness your vows to Mike, right?"

She nodded, dabbing at her pink nose.

"She will probably be upset with herself later if

she misses it, so you're really doing her a favor. If it will make you feel better, I'll make sure she knows she can leave right after the ceremony and avoid... whatshisname."

"Eric. He's her husband. Or was," she corrected immediately when he frowned. "They got divorced eighteen months ago, but they're both miserable," she rushed to add.

Trevor really didn't want to know about all that. Right now his mission was to make sure his buddy's wife-to-be was happy and ready to get married. He didn't want to think about the fact that he was meddling in anyone else's life, much less their love life. He'd personally guarantee Viv a ride home after the ceremony. Everyone would be happy.

He pushed the pencil and paper at Kate. She smiled through a fresh rush of tears. "Mike was right. You really are hero material. Thanks for saving my day." Her lip was trembling again. "Thank you so much for doing this."

Trevor nodded, silently praying for her to hurry with the directions so he could make his escape. When she handed the paper back, fingers trembling, he scanned the directions to make sure he could understand them. He'd lived in the area as a child and had been back when he could to see his grandmother, but she'd passed away years ago and his job with the Special Forces hadn't allowed him to come back very often since then. Things seemed to change every time he came back to this small suburb of Richmond, Virginia.

He gave Kate what he hoped was a reassuring nod. "Have your father tell the reverend to give me twenty minutes. I'll have her here ready to go."

...d Richmond. She'd...
...

1

CHRISTY RUSSELL was not a morning person. Or an afternoon, or middle-of-the-night person, either, depending on what shift she was working. She'd worked so many in a row now she'd totally lost track. All she knew was that she had no shifts of any kind for the next seventy-two hours. No pager, no cell phone, no emergency call ins. The world could come to an end and probably would given her luck, but she was not gracing the hallways of the Richmond General Hospital's ICU until Monday afternoon at four.

Three days. And she planned to remain unconscious for as much of the first one as possible.

And she would if they'd just stop that banging. Whoever "they" were. She grumbled in her sleep. Banging, banging, banging. She tossed one way, then yanked the covers over her head as she turned the other. Pound, pound and yelling. She wasn't going to listen to any yelling. Uh-uh. She was unconscious. Off work. Not available.

She sunk deeper into dreamland. Still, the noise followed. Someone calling for Viv. Ah, she thought hazily. Viv, not Christy. Good. She smiled and nestled into her pillow. No Viv. Viv gone, she remembered dreamily, then blocked the disturbance out once and for all by tugging her pillow over her head and sinking fully into the waiting arms of the Sandman.

"Get up, Vivian."

Mmm. The Sandman had a deep, sexy voice. She burrowed deeper under her pillows and blankets. Maybe he'd crawl into her dreams with her and bring that sexy voice with him. What else would go with such a sexy voice? she wondered dreamily.

"You're late for a very important date."

Date. Yeah. She'd go on a date with that voice. He sounded so real, so close. "C'mere," she murmured, mentally reaching for her dream man.

"Come on, wake up."

Strong hands. Yeah, they went very nicely with that voice. Strong, warm hands. A little rough, but then she could handle a demanding lover. Lord knew, it had been so long, she had a few demands of her own.

"Vivian, time to wake up. Now."

She frowned. "Viv?" she mumbled. Why did *her* dream man want Viv? That wasn't very nice. After all, *she'd* conjured him up, shouldn't he be wanting her? What kind of dream was this anyway?

"Vivian." Her dream man was becoming demanding, but not the way she'd like him to.

"Go 'way." She'd think up another dream man. It was bad enough she wasn't getting any action in real life, but she'd be damned if she'd put up with her own dream man choosing someone else over her.

And then her dream man was using those nice, strong hands to pull her covers off and yank her pillow away. *How rude!* Consciousness tugged at her, only her brain and most of her body weren't really willing to catch up. Which wasn't surprising given she was probably the world's heaviest sleeper.

"There's going to be a wedding in fifteen minutes and you're going to stand up for your best friend."

"Huh?" She had no idea what sort of whack dream this was, but she was really beginning to hate it. She flopped back on the bed and once again swore off convenience-store microwave tamales. Well, right before bed, anyway. They were one of her major food groups and she wasn't going to be so hasty as to swear off them forever. Food. Maybe she should dream about that....

"Oh, no, you don't."

She was being hauled upright again. This really must stop. She was sure she was telling him, but the words were all fuzzed up in her brain. All she wanted to do was sleep, dammit. Couldn't they just leave her alone to sleep? And just who the hell were *they* anyway?

She tried to struggle, but her arms were all sleep-gimpy and the Sandman was much stronger at any rate. "Whas going on? Hey!" This last came out much more clearly as she was unceremoniously dragged from her nice warm bed, or Viv's nice warm bed. Maybe that's why her dream man wanted Viv; it was her bed after all. Hmm... She began to drift again.

Then was awakened by her own shriek when she found herself turned almost upside down. "What the hell?" She blinked her eyes furiously, trying to clear the cobwebs. "What are you doing?" This demand was delivered directly to the very hard, very broad back of... Wait a minute. Her dream man wasn't real. Was he?

No, she must still be asleep after all. Okay, so no tamales *or* frozen cheesecake treats. Sheesh.

But she swiftly realized her predicament had nothing to do with sugar-and-spice overload. Because the warm, well-muscled forearm strapped across the back of her thighs was definitely real.

She began to struggle in earnest now as full consciousness was rudely and irrevocably thrust upon her. "Who the hell are you? Put me down!"

"Your best friend is crying her eyes out in a church on what should be the happiest day of her life and so you're going to put aside whatever personal problems you might have and go make her happy."

They were already heading down Viv's stairs and she grabbed his waist to keep her head from banging against his back. She couldn't string two coherent thoughts together, much less make any sense of what was happening to her. But one thing would certainly help. "Put. Me. Down."

But the hard body presently manhandling her wasn't remotely intimidated by her best ICU nurse voice. *Okay, okay,* she told herself. *Calm down, wake up, think, think.* What was he talking about? A wedding. Wedding.

"Oh! You must mean Kate Winchell."

"Nice of you to remember."

She finally put it together. He thought she was Vivian and Kate had sent him here to bring her matron of honor to the ceremony.

But the breath she'd planned to use to inform him of his dire mistake was oomphed out of her when he stepped off the front porch and headed toward a silver sedan. She forgot all about warning him when warm, humid air brushed her legs. Her very bare legs. *Oh my God!* "Wait just a damn minute! I don't have any clothes on!"

She heard a rustle of plastic. "I've got them. You can dress at the church."

"But I'm not—"

"Save the excuses. Whatever they are, you can swallow them for the twenty minutes it's going to take for my buddy to marry the love of his life." He shifted her as easily as a sack of potatoes so he could open the door. "A woman with apparently lousy taste in best friends," he added, clearly disgusted. "But she deserves a nice wedding day and I'm going to make sure she gets it."

Christy was dumped in the front seat of the car, quite rudely she thought, and was just winding up to deliver a blistering speech to enlighten this...this Neanderthal Kate had apparently sent to get Vivian. But all the words and a goodly amount of the venom she'd been building since the moment he tossed her over his shoulder died in her throat the instant she came face-to-face with him.

He was very possibly the most gorgeous Neanderthal she'd ever laid eyes on.

And speaking of eyes. At the moment, his were mere inches away from hers as he leaned in to get the seat-belt harness. They were blue. Lord, were they ever. All the poetic words ever used on a greeting card couldn't describe just how blue those eyes were.

She opened her mouth, then closed it again. Better not to speak until she was sure she wouldn't drool. Not that she could be any more humiliated at this point. No makeup, puffy eyes, bed hair...and wearing white cotton underwear. *Oh, yeah, she was a real temptress.* Not that she wanted to tempt the guy. But her body didn't seem willing to register that reality. Oh, no, her body was exceedingly aware that white cotton or not, she wasn't wearing very much of it. And his hands were hovering close to...well, close to places she really shouldn't want a stranger's hands to hover. But she wanted them to anyway.

God, she was tired. That had to be the reason she waited until the last possible second before smacking his hands away and taking the seat belt from him. One second later and his knuckles would have grazed...well, she didn't want to think about what those knuckles would have been grazing against. Her nipples were thinking about it far too much already, thank you very much.

"Buckle up," he said tersely and stepped back, apparently oblivious to the near riot he'd created with her hormones.

Sleep deprivation—she was sure that was the only reason they were all in a dither. That and a severe lack of love life. Tough combination, and after the eyeful she got watching him as he straightened, she decided she couldn't really blame her nipples one bit.

He locked her door and shut it tightly, making her flinch. *Venom buildup returning,* she thought, scowling as she watched him walk with a rigid preciseness that made the military uniform he wore seem redundant. But damn, if he didn't fill that uniform out. And men in uniform didn't even make the top ten on her list of things to fantasize about. "Well, that could change," she murmured, mind wandering. Of course, in her fantasies the man in uniform wouldn't be a rude, Neanderthal, hormone-inducing jerk. Well, except for the hormone-inducing part. That would probably be okay. And those eyes, those would work.

God, she was punchy. How had she let this happen anyway? Yawning fiercely, she let her head drop back on the headrest. She knew Kate Winchell, but only through Viv. Christy had met her fiancé, Mike, at a July Fourth picnic once. He was a former Special Forces guy, she couldn't remember with what part of the military, but given the uniform, she guessed this was one of his pals. Her eyelids drooped and her mind was tugged back toward dreamland as she vaguely wondered if she and her blue-eyed Neanderthal Man would have hit it off if they'd met at a picnic. Maybe he'd wear that uniform...and let her take it off later, alone. Somewhere where they could have their own private display of fireworks. Oh, yeah, that would be great....

She almost leaped out of her skin when he slammed his door shut. Which put him inside the car. Right next to her. Her and her rioting, fantasizing hormones. And her barely clad body. She hunched down a little and shifted toward the door, not that he hadn't already seen everything. And it didn't make a bit of difference, nor did the fact that her brain knew she'd never give this guy the time of day after the way he'd treated her. Her body was still back at her fantasy picnic, getting ready to explode a few fireworks.

Okay, so she'd been pulling too many double shifts. She had school loans to pay off and a fixer-upper condo that was turning into a money pit of nightmare proportions. She had priorities. And they didn't include fireworks. In or out of uniform.

But her gaze slid over to him anyway. Along his thighs, so nicely outlined in his crisp dress pants, to the belted jacket that covered...well, things she didn't need to be visualizing as she was overstimulated enough at the moment. But she didn't look away. No, she had to look at his hands...and oh, Lord, what hands they were.

She might not have men-in-uniform fantasies, but she definitely had a thing about hands. And his were...perfect. Wide palms, long fingers, blunt nails, all capable and strong as they gripped the leather-wrapped steering wheel. They'd be just as strong and capable gripping her hips. She tried not to squirm, tried not to imagine. But perhaps, just maybe, her priorities needed readjusting a tiny bit.

The man just kidnapped you from your own bed for chrissakes!

She jerked her gaze back to the passenger window. She had no right fantasizing about this guy. So what if he thought she was someone else? Breaking and entering, kidnapping...all those things were still against the law. And just because Kate was sniffling, well, she shouldn't have set Viv up to begin with! Christy should be furious, not fantasizing!

The headache she'd almost medicated away earlier crawled back inside her head with renewed force. She needed to be in bed and there was a perfectly good one not fifty yards away. So what in the hell was she doing letting this guy drag her to an event she hadn't even been invited to?

She turned to face Mr. Gorgeous Neanderthal Man and tell him just that, but just as abruptly decided against it. Oh, no, there was a much better way for him to learn of his giant faux pas. Swallowing a smile, she leaned back in the plush leather seat, deciding to just enjoy the short ride to the chapel. He'd learn soon enough that he'd plundered the wrong bed. Or the wrong woman anyway. She let her eyes drift shut as she imagined the humiliation payback that was going to be his when they pulled up in front of the chapel and— "Oh my God!" Her eyes flew open.

He hit the brakes. "What?"

"I'm not wearing anything!" Which she already knew. What she hadn't factored in was that they were heading to a church where everyone else would find out she was only wearing her underwear.

He scowled and resumed his race to the church. "If you'd been here with everyone else, you wouldn't have this problem."

Christy didn't waste breath explaining the mix-up to him. Being a nurse, she'd worked with her share of arrogant men in her life. The man next to her was the military equivalent. He'd already assessed the situation, made his diagnosis—and nothing this lowly nurse had to say was going to change his decided method of treatment.

So she attacked the one part of the problem that dealt directly with her own well-being. "You are not depositing me on a street corner in my underwear. Nor will you be hauling me into a church in front of anyone in my underwear."

"Then I suggest you haul your fanny over the seat and start getting dressed." He didn't even look at her. Or her fanny.

Not that she wanted him to, of course.

"Better get a move on. We'll be there in three minutes."

She had to curl her fingers against the very real urge to smack his chiseled, too-damn-good-looking profile. *You're a nurse. You heal, not hurt.* At that particular moment, she really wanted to make an exception to that rule.

However, as she was faced with an extremely embarrassing situation, she didn't waste any more time. She scrambled over the seat, swallowing her mortification as various parts of her body brushed far too close to various parts of his body, namely his face. All he had to do was turn his head and—

She made an ungraceful dive for the back seat, landing in a most unladylike sprawl. Not that he'd noticed any of it. Or any of her. Coldhearted bastard. *She'd* certainly noticed. Her pulse was pounding and not entirely in frustration. She gave in to the impulse to stick her tongue out at the back of his head, then looked with great trepidation at the melon-colored, sequin-and-chiffon creation that awaited her. Dear God, she thought. What on earth had Viv's friend been thinking? It looked for all the world like an overpriced Las Vegas fruit salad.

But it was either dress like a glazed melon ball or face Kate, the assembled wedding party and every rubbernecker on the road in front of the church in her underwear.

Someday you'll laugh about all this, she told herself, tearing the plastic bag off the dress. But as she squeezed her curvy size-twelve body into Viv's narrow, size-ten dress, she had an increasingly hard time believing anything about this day would ever remotely amuse her.

2

TREVOR GRIPPED the steering wheel as if his life depended on it, forcing himself to keep his eyes on the road and not the mirrored reflection of what was taking place in the back seat of his rental sedan.

Dear Lord, but that woman had curves on top of curves. He felt sweat bead up on his forehead and knew it had nothing to do with the summer humidity. What had he been thinking making her climb over that seat? She'd all but smothered his ear with...with body parts that hadn't been rubbed against his ear in...well, maybe never. Not that he wasn't an adventurous lover, or willing to be, but—Jesus, his ear felt like it was on fire. Good damn thing she hadn't brushed up against anything else.

He still remembered the silky smooth feel of her legs under his hands. Of course, he'd been busy trying to ignore the combustible reaction she'd set off inside him when he'd pulled her half-naked, very warm and pliable body out of that bed. She'd draped herself over him like a warm blanket. Okay, so she'd been unconscious, but his body didn't care about that!

Damn Kate and her stupid reunion scheme. He

made the last turn and glanced in the rearview mirror as the church loomed into view. He was lucky he didn't put the car in a ditch. Did she have any idea what she looked like in that dress? It fit like a second skin, and there was cleavage…everywhere.

This was a wedding, not Hugh Hefner's latest bunny roundup. Had Kate really okayed that getup? Weren't all eyes supposed to be on the bride? Because with all that exposed flesh in the front and her well-rounded backside being showcased just as outrageously, no warm-blooded male in his right mind was going to be looking anywhere else for the duration of the ceremony. Her shoulder-length hair was a wild swirl of brunette curls that would be a rat's nest on any other woman, but coupled with those pouty lips and heavy-lidded, dark chocolate eyes…and that dress, she looked like sex incarnate.

Why in the hell would Kate allow herself to be upstaged like this? Or had she okayed the dress in hopes her pal would use hormone overload to win her ex-husband back? Of course, at the moment Trevor thought the man had been insane to let her get away in the first place.

"I just want you to know you're about to make the biggest mistake of your life. And I'm going to enjoy every minute of it," she said, eyes flashing, smile a tad smug.

Okay, so maybe this Eric had been wiser than he gave him credit for. Vivian conjured all kinds of slinky, feline comparisons…including the sharp claws and teeth.

"Don't pull any fast ones," he warned, not that she could in that dress. He wasn't sure how she was going to walk in it, much less run away.

He pulled up right in front of the church, parking behind the limo with Just Married painted on the rear window. The bridesmaids were probably already lined up, so she could just slip into the front and no one would know she was making a forced appearance. Kate could take it from there and he'd thankfully head to his place at the head of the chapel next to his buddy. He said a silent prayer for the pile of trouble Mike was about to marry. And a silent apology to Eric, as well. He'd never met the man, but he didn't relish the reunion he was in for.

He patted his pocket as he unbuckled and got out, breathing a sigh of relief. Ring box was still there. An hour from now he'd be toasting the bride and groom and this whole ordeal would be over.

He went to open the back door, but Vivian had already swung it open and was trying to maneuver her way out. However, the snug fit of the dress was restricting her movement to the point that getting out without assistance would be mission impossible. He pushed her hands away—twice—and hauled her out.

"I can manage," she ground out.

"Yes, ma'am."

She made a face and he found himself stifling a smile. Definitely a handful. Several handfuls, in fact, he thought as he carefully set her on her tottering heels. His actions had caused her dress to roll dangerously high, well past her knees. The cut was so low in the front that she didn't dare lean down to fix the hem for fear of spilling out of it.

Glaring at him, she simply motioned him to fix it. For some reason her autocratic, silent demand tweaked at him. "Do you require further assistance, ma'am?"

"You know damn well I do. It's all your fault I'm even here, so the least you can do is make this horrid outfit as presentable as possible."

Only years of intensive training saved him from laughing out loud. "So you didn't pick this out yourself?"

She bared her teeth into what might pass for a smile. On a tiger. "Pull the hem down. Please." This last was added as if under extreme duress.

And looking at the way her curves were strapped into way too little fabric, he realized she probably was. "Yes, ma'am." He knelt in front of her and tried, really tried, not to notice the smooth expanse of leg in front of him, or how it had felt beneath his fingertips.

She twitched as he gingerly took hold of the thin fabric and tugged. She twitched again and made a strange gargling sound. No way was he lifting his head to check on her, however. "Be still. This thing isn't giving."

She snorted again, then snickered and finally swatted at him to stop. "Stop, stop, you're killing me here."

He did look up then. Big mistake. "Beg—" He

had to clear his throat…and his vision of the bounty of cleavage in front of him. "Beg your pardon?"

"I'm ticklish, okay? And you're being awfully damn polite for a kidnapper." He opened his mouth to argue, but she talked over him. "Just leave the dress alone. It's not like I'm going to have it on for very long."

Perfectly happy to follow orders this go around, Trevor stood and eyed her, but thought it best not to respond to that last comment. But, oh, the lucky man who got to peel that dress off of her, he couldn't help thinking. Providing he could find a way to keep her mouth shut, that is.

"Well, best to get this over with," she said, but when she went to take a step, they both realized the dress wasn't that flexible. Nor were the spiky heels that appeared wedged on her feet.

Trevor sighed, but time was wasting and Mike was probably getting a bit worried about his best man. He didn't even want to think what shape Kate was in. So he did what he had to do. He scooped her up in his arms, ignored her squeal of protest—and the way her breasts all but heaved out of the front of the dress—and carried her up the stairs of the church.

"You are so going to regret this," she said. "And if I weren't so busy trying to breathe, I'd probably enjoy it."

Trevor tapped the door of the church with his shoe and focused straight ahead. He really must have been overseas too long, because just the sweet pressure of her sequin-clad fanny against the front of his body was enough to make him very glad his dress uniform included a long jacket. He tapped the door with a bit more force.

Finally it cracked open, revealing a sea of melon sequins, teased hair and flower bouquets. Trevor was tempted to just shove her inside and make a run for it, but Kate emerged through the throng like a white-chiffon swan.

"Thank goodness! I was worried I'd lost my matron of honor and Mike's best man!" She sounded giddy bordering on hysterical as the sequin-and-satin sea parted to allow him to enter. Kate's giddiness dissolved the instant she spied the woman in his arms. "Who is that? Christy?" She raised glassy eyes to Trevor. "What's going on here?"

"Christy?" Trevor repeated helplessly.

The woman in his arms smiled sweetly at him, and bent her fingers in a little wave. "That would be me."

"But— *Holy*—" Trevor bit off the oath, conscious of his surroundings. He was usually able to control his temper; in fact his job demanded he keep his cool under the most trying circumstances. But his special ops training hadn't prepared him for neurotic brides, AWOL bridesmaids...and sleeping beauties.

He set his jaw and carefully placed the woman in his arms on her feet. "I went to the address you provided and picked up—"

"Kidnapped," Christy corrected.

"Picked up," he repeated, "the one and only female resident, whom I naturally presumed to be Vivian, and brought her here as you requested."

Kate immediately swung her tear-filled gaze to the woman wobbling next to him. He reached out to help steady her, but was glared into withdrawing his offer of assistance. Fine, he'd just leave them to it, then. Except he couldn't. He'd brought her here and had refused to listen to any explanations on her part. At the very least he owed it to her to stand by until the situation was resolved.

"Why didn't you tell him you weren't Vivian?" Kate demanded, her bevy of bridesmaids watching the exchange as avidly as fans at a tennis match.

Christy folded her arms, then thought better of it when her chest came dangerously close to spilling forth. "I tried, believe me."

But Kate was losing it completely and didn't seem to hear. "And why are you wearing Vivian's dress? I can't let you go into the chapel dressed like that."

Trevor had to bite off the surprising urge to smile when he saw Christy's hackles all but rise off the back of her neck. *Well, this should be good.* He was guilty as all hell in this matter, but he'd make his apologies after the firestorm died down. In the meantime, Christy looked fully capable of delivering the speech about what happens when people intrude on other people's lives. A lesson he needed to learn only once.

"Oh, I have no intention of going into that chapel. But your hired hound didn't allow me the luxury of getting dressed before he kidnapped me from my bed. Or Vivian's bed." She waved a dismissive hand, making him duck or get smacked. "So I put on the only thing available."

"Well, I'm very sorry you were dragged here unnecessarily, but I had no idea you were at Viv's house. Where is Viv?" she demanded.

Now Christy's eyes narrowed. "You must be crazy if you think I'm telling you that. If she wanted to be here and let you manipulate her life after you swore you wouldn't, she'd be here. Trust me, it cost her plenty to walk away from her obligation to you, but when you went back on your word, I didn't see any reason for her to keep her word."

"*You* didn't?" Kate took a step forward, but her dress prevented her from coming any closer. "You told her about Eric? How did you find out?"

"Eric happened to make the unfortunate assumption that I would back your little scheme and wanted me to help make sure Viv went to the reception. I, on the other hand, totally championed her desire to get away from the whole affair." Christy immediately calmed down when Kate began to cry in earnest.

Trevor watched her exhale a weary sigh and for the first time noticed the fatigue clear in the depths of her dark eyes. The heavy-lidded eyes and puffy lips he'd attributed to a sort of exotic beauty were in fact signs of a bone-deep weariness, which made him feel like a complete heel. She had been sound asleep in the middle of the day for a good reason apparently. He, on the other hand, had no good reason for handling things as poorly as he had.

Christy took a wobbling step forward and placed a hand on Kate's arm. "Listen, I know your heart was in the right place," she said gently, "but you shouldn't have interfered. I'm really sorry. I'm sure you two can patch this up when you get back from your honeymoon." She rubbed Kate's arm, surprising Trevor with her sincerity considering her own treatment today. "You have a man in there who loves you and wants to marry you," she went on. "That's what this day is all about. There will be time later to sort the rest out. Trust me."

Kate sniffled. "You think she'll forgive me?"

Christy nodded confidently and gave her a little nudge, almost falling over when Kate smiled and moved away from her toward the door to the chapel at the same moment.

Trevor's quick reflexes saved Christy from diving facefirst into Kate's train.

"I'm really sorry about the misunderstanding," Kate called out over her shoulder.

Christy just waved her off, her smile evaporating as soon as she turned to face Trevor. "Shouldn't you be inside helping your buddy get married?" She eyed his hand on her arm, then looked up at him.

"That was nice, what you just did for her. She didn't deserve the kindness and neither do I. But I'd like to try and—"

"Listen, save the apologies until after the ceremony. You can grovel when you drive me home on your way to the reception, okay?"

Trevor didn't know whether to laugh or swear. She'd handled this a lot better than most women would, and though he felt like a total ass and planned to tell her so, he suddenly found himself in no hurry to leave her. "Where will you be?"

She smiled dryly. "Leaning on whatever wall you prop me up against."

"Maybe I can find you something more suitable to wear?"

The organ music paused, then made them both jump as it suddenly resumed with the thundering opening strains of the bridal march. "No time for that. Get in there and do your thing. I'll be fine."

Trevor felt even worse that she was being such a good sport about this. She must have read his mind, because her smile brought back those feline comparisons...the ones with bared teeth and claws.

"However, if you come back to find me sleeping standing up, it's on your head if you wake me again. And you already have quite enough on your head at the moment, if you know what I mean. I hope you grovel as well as you kidnap."

"I've never had to grovel before, but I'm sure I'll come up with something." He helped her away from the throng of bridesmaids queuing up to go inside the chapel, over to a far corner, away from the front door, as well. "Are you sure—"

"I'm sure," she cut in, eyes already drooping shut.

"What if you took off the shoes? Would that—"

"They're strapped on. Just go," she said, not bothering to open her eyes.

He should. He knew that. But he really didn't want to. "Christy—"

"Please," she ordered.

He had no idea where the impulse came from, or why he gave in to it. God knew his impulses had already caused enough problems today. And he'd thought civilian life would be easier! But he was already reaching for the loose tendrils of hair that clung to her cheeks and pushing them back.

Her eyes flew open at the feel of his fingers brushing against her cheek. "What are you doing?"

He grinned then and enjoyed the way her pupils shot wide and her throat worked. "Wishing we'd met under just about any other circumstances." Before she could say anything to make him regret that little announcement, he gave her a sharp salute. "I'll be back as soon as possible." And headed down the side hallway toward the altar door.

3

CHRISTY TRIED to doze, but she couldn't get those blue eyes out of her mind. Why did he have to go and touch her like that anyway? Despite what her hormones thought, she was really fully prepared to not like the guy. After what he'd put her through, how hard should that be?

She squirmed and shifted her weight what little she could without tipping over. This dress was a pain to be sure, but the heels were instruments of torture that would make the Marquis de Sade weep with pleasure. She, on the other hand, just wanted to weep. She wished now she'd agreed to let— She realized she didn't even know his name!

The organ came to life again, making her wince. But it was only when the chapel doors were pushed wide to allow the newly married couple to emerge that she thought about exactly what would happen next. The bridesmaids and groomsmen would follow...and then every single person in the church would come out behind them. Right past her. In this dress.

She looked frantically around for some sort of camouflage, but knew one step would send her sprawling. Why hadn't she thought this through before letting whatever his name was leave her here, propped against the wall like some party favor blow-up doll? Maybe he'd realize it and as soon as he came through the door with the maid of honor— Except there was no maid of honor. So she had no idea where he was in the ensemble at this point.

Kate and Mike emerged through the doors just then in a cloud of white chiffon and flowers. They only had eyes for each other, and even as Christy did her best to become one with the wall, she couldn't ignore the lump that rose in her throat. She *was* happy for them, just as she'd been happy for Vivian three years before.

And look where that had ended up, her inner voice mocked. She only hoped Mike had the fortitude to put up with Kate. God, did she sound like a cynical old maid or what? She wasn't that bad, was she? She was only twenty-eight for heaven's sake. Hardly over the hill. *How can you ever marry if you never date?* Her mother's oft-repeated words echoed inside her head. She'd never paid attention to them, knowing her mother would only go from wanting weddings to wanting grandbabies, and she was in no hurry to do either.

But she *was* twenty-eight. With thirty on the horizon. And no prospects. The bridesmaids started out the door and Christy shrank even farther back, knowing the assembled guests were next, praying they'd keep their eyes straight ahead. She didn't want prospects, she told herself. She had a demanding job she loved and if someone came along who demanded her attention in the same way, fine. But that hadn't happened. So what if logic dictated she had to actually be looking in order to meet someone? She certainly wasn't going to hunt down a guy just because all her friends were getting married.

They were also getting divorced, she reminded herself. Well, Vivian had anyway. And if there had ever been a couple who seemed meant for one another, it was those two. And yet, there they were, miserable and alone. Why should she be in any hurry to become another statistic?

She was actually doing the wise thing, focusing on her own life, her career and not searching for love. If love wanted her attention, it would just have to find her.

"You ready to go?"

His deep voice vibrated just behind her ear, so low and sexy it sent shivers of awareness throughout her entire, shrink-wrapped body. Okay, so she wasn't looking for love, but an afternoon of mindless sex was sure sounding pretty good at the moment. And oh, did he sound good. Better than good. He sounded like—

Horrified at the sudden direction of her thoughts, she stiffened, which immediately lost her the support of the wall...and pitched her directly into the support of his lean, hard body.

He immediately folded her against him, steadying them both, but rather than stand her back upright, he scooped her into his arms.

"No!" she rasped, looking frantically about, certain they were drawing stares. But the crowd was pushing as one out the front doors, and before she could protest further, she was being whisked away, down the side hallway, mercifully out of sight. "Thank you," she said sincerely, if a bit breathlessly. That last part was due to the dress cutting off her air supply, not because of the feel of his body pressed against her. She was certain of it.

He put her down near the door to the rear parking lot of the church. "Wait here."

He was so close, his body felt so nice and hard against hers…she all but swooned against him.

"Steady," was all he said, then carefully propped her in a corner and disappeared behind a white paneled door without another glance.

Well, she thought, scowling at the now-vacant spot beside her. Apparently she was the only one suffering from hormone shock. She definitely had to forget those blue eyes looking into hers while he told her he wished they'd met under different circumstances. They hadn't. And even if she was willing to forgive him—and she wasn't saying she was—the rental car made it clear he was not a permanent fixture around here, or anywhere if the uniform meant anything. She let her eyes slide shut. And Lord, he was a man meant to wear a uniform. Protecting lives and making the world a safer place. A bubble of laughter pushed up her throat. Unless of course you were a bridesmaid ditching your pal's wedding. Then he was a dangerous man.

She thought about the way he'd taken her out of the house. Yes, he might be charming and polite when he wanted to be, but there was no doubt that he was a man who got what he wanted, when he wanted it.

The door popped open again and he was back, taking up way too much of her personal space and invading her emotional comfort zone just as effortlessly. She, on the other hand, apparently hadn't made the least little dent in his. He handed her what looked like a long white gown.

"Choir robe," he said. "I thought you might want to get out of that dress before we left."

Visions of him doing just that came right into her mind without even asking permission. She shoved them aside and hugged the robe to her chest. "Thank you." Then she realized she hadn't completed her descent into Bridesmaid Hell. "Um... apparently I'm going to need some help getting this thing off."

Where other men might have drooled openly at the opportunity to help any woman out of her clothes, he actually looked uncomfortable. She could almost like him for that.

"You didn't seem to have the least compunction in carrying me out of my house in my underwear," she reminded him, even as her little voice told her it wasn't wise to goad the man. What did her little voice know anyway? It hadn't kept her out of this mess in the first place, now had it?

"Is there a...zipper or something?" he asked,

looking her over as if her dress was some sort of secret military weapon.

If she hadn't been so tired and uncomfortable, she might have enjoyed making him sweat a little. It was the least he deserved. "I rolled it on basically."

He just stared at her. Now it was her turn to feel a bit uncomfortable. Okay, more than a little. Having his hands on her, pulling this dress off— *You're in a church, for heaven's sake,* she reminded herself. She cleared her throat. "We should probably hurry up. Don't you have to be in the pictures or something?"

"They're taking the group photos at the country club."

"Well, then let's get this over with so you can drop me off and be on your way."

He knelt in front of her, lifted his hands to the hem that was still scrunched up around her knees, then dropped them again. "I'm, uh, not sure where to begin."

She carefully held her arms out and delivered her best smile. Maybe making him sweat was going to be more fun than she thought. "I think the Band-Aid approach is best. Just yank."

He looked up at her then and she felt her stomach drop and her heart begin to pound. Here she was, standing in a church, in a fancy dress, with a gorgeous man on one knee in front of her. Scowling. She couldn't get anything right.

"Hold on to my shoulders," he directed. "If I can roll this up a bit, maybe then you can, you know, take it from there."

His hands, with those long fingers...all up and down her thighs. Jesus, she'd never survive it without disgracing herself. But then, that wasn't much of a stretch at the moment, was it? "Okay, okay." She took a deep breath, or as deep a one as the dress would allow. "But close your eyes."

He grabbed hold of the hem and shoved upward, but the fabric stopped just below crotch level, bound tightly around her hips. She wobbled and came dangerously close to pitching forward, which would have pressed his face...well, right where no man should have his face when inside a church. "Stop, stop," she said breathlessly. "Get me out of these shoes." She should have done that first anyway.

He did, all warm fingertips brushing at her skin, sending a tingling sensation all the way up to...well, where his face had almost been moments ago. Who knew ankles were erogenous zones?

She came dangerously close to moaning when she felt his warm breath on her skin as his fingers slid around her ankle to unbuckle one shoe, then the other. As it was, she had to sink her nails more deeply into his uniformed shoulders just to remain upright.

"Hold on, one more buckle. Got it." He stood carefully, apparently oblivious to the near orgasm he'd just given her.

She really did need to get to bed. Alone, she quickly amended as she stepped gingerly and oh-so-very thankfully out of the instruments of death.

She'd never been so glad to feel the ground so firm and cold beneath her toes. "Okay, here's the plan," she said, trying hard to focus on just getting out of the shrink-wrap with as little touching on his part as possible. "I'm going to put the robe on and pull the shoulder straps off and roll the dress down to my waist. Then I'll push and you pull and the whole thing should drop off, right?"

He looked dubious.

"It's that or cut the damn thing off. I'd rather not do that to Viv's dress. Who knows, maybe she can get a refund or...or something. Let's just try, okay?"

"Yes, ma'am."

"Great. And stop ma'aming me. Makes me feel like an old granny or something."

He grinned then, just before dropping the robe over her head. "Trust me," he said, his voice muffled by the voluminous folds of white cotton. "You're nothing like any grandmother I've ever seen. It's just habit. Military."

She wisely said nothing as she squirmed out of the dress straps, keeping her arms inside the robe. She'd shrugged out of her tank top straps when she'd put this monstrosity on, and tucked them inside the dress. But she couldn't untuck them now. Why should that surprise her? She tried to tug the top part down, but while the front part was willing—her boobs were thrilled to finally be free—the sides and back were all hung up with the cotton of her undershirt.

"Should I tug now?"

"Just a minute." She tugged a scrap of tank top from the front and held on tight to it. "Close your eyes."

She felt his fingertips brush her thighs again. "Eyes closed," he said.

She realized hers were, too. "On three. One, two—now!"

She gripped, he yanked...and the dress gave way and fell to the floor. Right along with her panties.

"Just, uh, just turn around, okay? I can take it from here."

She opened her eyes as he stood, gulping a little when he seemed suddenly so much taller than before. The heels, she realized. She was not a small woman and it was odd to feel so...petite. Well, not that she'd ever be described as petite, but maybe it was all relative.

"You okay? You look a little flushed."

"Oxygen deprivation," she quipped, not bothering to tell him that he, and not the dress, was more to blame for that little problem. She shifted and stood over the pool of sequins...and her panties. "I...um..." Damn, but his eyes were piercing. "Could you...turn around?"

He grinned. "Yes, ma'am."

She made a face at his back. It was that or smile. And was that uniform padded, or were his shoulders really that broad? They filled her entire line of vision. But she'd had her hands on those shoulders. They were all his.

She hastily pulled on her panties and scooped up

the pile of sequins and silk, along with the strappy heels. Clutching the billowy robe against her, she said, "I'm ready." He turned to face her and all she could think was, *Boy, am I ever*. Sleep. She desperately needed sleep.

He held out an arm, all spit and polish and blazing baby blues. "I had someone bring my car around back. It's right outside the door here. I'll take you directly home."

She wasn't sure she should touch any part of him. She wanted to, though. So much so that she gestured in front of them instead. "Lead on."

He moved to open her door, but she scooted in front of him, climbed in and all but lunged for the seat belt. "I got it." She reached for the door handle and yanked the door shut in his face. She didn't even care if it seemed rude. Lord knows he deserved worse, she told herself, no matter how charming and polite he was being now. But no way was he going to touch her again. Sleep. That was what she was going to focus on.

She let her head drop on the back of the seat and closed her eyes, pretending she didn't know he'd climbed in beside her, all big and warm, with those long fingers wrapped around that steering wheel.

"Listen, I really do want to apologize."

"Just get me in bed and all is forgiven." As soon as the words left her mouth, she realized how they sounded. Her eyes popped open and she sat up straight. "I mean—"

He glanced at her and smiled. "I know what you meant."

She opened her mouth, realized saying anything right now would just make it worse, and let her head drop back again.

He remained mercifully silent on the short ride back to Vivian's. She was drifting off to sleep when he pulled into the driveway.

"Christy?"

She stifled a yawn and blinked her eyes open. "Here already?" She was so tired she wasn't sure she'd make it to the bed. Of course, no way was she letting him know that.

"You did want to come back here, right?"

She nodded. "I'm having the floors redone at my place and they didn't get the sanding done on time, so they were still staining and sealing them when I got home...whatever day it was. I've lost track. Vivian let me bunk here."

"You're obviously beat and it's my fault I've kept you from catching up on your sleep. I am sincerely sorry."

She smiled to herself. She was daydreaming about him carrying her off in his arms...and he was telling her she looked about as delectable as day-old bread. Ah, reality. "I know Kate can make even the sanest person go a little nuts when she gets a plan in her head. She should be the one apologizing. To all of us."

"Let me help you inside."

"No!" At his surprised look, she calmed down

and smiled. "I can take it from here." She put her hand on the door. "Just how did you get in anyway? Or is that just part of military training?"

"Back door was unlocked. You'd better tell your friend Viv to be more careful about that."

"She wasn't exactly thinking clearly when she cut out of here." She sighed then. "I hope she's okay."

"Can't you call her and tell her the coast is clear?"

"She's up at her parent's lake house. She's planning on staying the weekend and it's probably just as well. If Eric flew in for the reception then he's likely staying through tomorrow anyway."

Just then there was a light tap on a horn and they both turned in time to see a car pull into the drive behind them.

"Oh, great. And here I thought the day couldn't possibly get any worse."

"Who is that?"

A tall, blond man climbed out from the car. Dressed in an impeccably cut suit, his hair just as impeccably trimmed. He went directly toward the house, a sense of purpose clear on his handsome face.

Trevor was already opening his door. Christy swore and leaped out of the car first. "Eric, wait."

4

ERIC SPUN AROUND. "Christy. Don't try and stop me. I have to talk to Vivian."

Christy almost tripped over her robe as she scooted between Eric and— She realized she still had no idea what her abductor's name was. She looked at him. "What is your name anyway?"

He came to a halt. "What?"

"Where's Vivian?" Eric demanded. "And why are you dressed like that?"

She looked back to Eric. "It's a long story. But I don't—"

"I never told you my—?" Trevor broke off with a smile and shake of his head, then grinned and saluted her. "Former Lieutenant Commander Trevor McQuillen, at your service."

"I don't care who the hell you are," Eric interjected.

"Well, perhaps you should care," Trevor said, pushing past Christy, who grabbed hold of his arm at the last second.

"Wait a minute!" she shouted, her head pounding in earnest now. "Just stop, both of you."

She turned to Trevor. "Thank you for bringing me

home. You should probably get to the reception. They'll be wondering." She swung back to Eric, well aware that Trevor hadn't so much as budged. "Vivian isn't here."

"I was at the church when the wedding party came out," he said. "She wasn't there. I thought I asked you to help me out, make sure she didn't run."

"No, you *told* me what I was supposed to do. Just like you told Vivian she was supposed to leave her friends and family, sell the house you'd just bought, give up her job and move halfway around the world because you thought you had an exciting job offer. No promise of stability, no thought of what she wanted or what was important to her. Oh nooo, you were Mr. Breadwinner. She trusted you to treat her as an equal, Eric, to love her and respect her as much as she did you. And you blew it. So you think you'd have learned by now that the world doesn't revolve around what Eric wants."

Eric swore, then raked a hand through his hair. "I'm sorry."

"I don't think it's fair to put Christy in the middle of this," Trevor offered, then rolled his eyes and backed off when they both glared at him. "Fine, fine. Just trying to help."

"Yeah, and we all know how successful you are at helping," Christy said.

Trevor smiled. "Okay, I deserved that. But believe it or not, I've actually run many successful operations in my career."

"This isn't a military operation, it's a wedding."

"Yes, and I'm learning that some of our military leaders might learn a thing or two about battle strategy from America's brides."

"Very funny."

"I wasn't kidding."

Christy tried not to smile, really she did. But when he wasn't dragging unsuspecting women from their beds, he could actually be somewhat charming.

And still dangerous. Because the instant she let her guard down, he was moving closer. And she was having a hard time remembering why that wasn't a good thing. Charmed and dangerous, that was Trevor McQuillen.

He stood right in front of her, blocking her vision of everything but him. "I *am* sorry about this, Christy."

"You said that already."

"Maybe I can make it up to you. Somehow."

Her heart sped up. "I—you'll be leaving soon."

He pushed a strand of hair behind her ear. "Says who?"

She all but shuddered in pleasure as his fingertips grazed her cheek. "Your uniform. Your rental car."

"I—"

"Listen, I just want to know where my wife is," Eric said, stepping between them.

"Ex-wife," Christy snapped at him, then stepped back herself. Her emotions were all in a whirl. She was too tired to deal with all this.

Trevor turned and subtly maneuvered Eric several steps away as he spoke. "Why don't you follow me over to the reception? This is Kate's and Mike's day. I'm sure you can come to some solution with Vivian after this is over."

"I wouldn't bet on it," Christy said mutinously.

Eric turned back to her, even as Trevor took his arm in a firm grip. "Where is she, Christy?" Eric begged. "I just want to talk to her. If she tells me to take a hike, I will."

"Yeah, well, you'll be making a long one if you want to see her again."

Eric's eyes lit up and Christy could have kicked herself for the slip.

"She's gone to the lake, hasn't she?"

Christy kept her lips firmly shut, but she knew it was too late. The only good thing was that Eric had never been to the cabin. It belonged to Vivian's parents. They'd just finished building it right when Eric and Viv split up. Viv had gone up to the lake because she knew he couldn't contact her there.

"Christy—"

"Eric, come on, man," Trevor said, his tone genial enough, but his expression implacable. "Let's go to the reception."

Eric started to argue, then decided better of it. "Okay, okay." He pulled his arm free. "You're right."

Christy was instantly suspicious. Eric was nothing if not determined. It was why he was so successful in his career—and why he'd failed so miserably in marriage. Some things can't be achieved with bull determination.

"I'm sorry I involved you in this," Eric told her. "But...I was desperate."

He looked it, she had to admit. In fact, despite his perfect hair, perfect clothes and perfect face...there was no mistaking the misery in his eyes. She didn't doubt he was sorry he'd lost Viv. It was the only thing he'd ever failed at and it was simply unacceptable for Eric Swenson to fail at anything.

"Please, when you talk to her, just tell her that all I want is the chance to talk, to explain. I've changed, Christy."

"Not from where I'm standing," she said, but with more sadness than anger. She felt bad for both of them, but she also knew her friend had been devastated by the failure of her marriage and she didn't want to see Viv put through any more hell.

"Christy, I—"

"I think we'd better leave," Trevor interjected.

Eric looked as if he was going to resist, but he sighed and nodded. "Okay. I'm sorry, Christy," he said again and walked back toward his car.

She turned to Trevor. "Thank you."

"He seems pretty sincere. Are you sure—?" He broke off when Christy folded her arms and glared at him. "Right, right. I think I've butted in enough for one day." He laughed. "Civilian life was supposed to be easier."

"You're out of the military now?"

He nodded. "The uniform is for the wedding

only. I'm starting my own defensive training facility just north of here."

"Here?" He wasn't leaving. He was going to be...around. Christy wasn't sure how she felt about that. Her body, however, knew exactly how *it* felt.

"I used to live here." He looked around and sighed. "Feels like a million years ago."

Christy was undeniably intrigued. He couldn't be much past thirty, if that, and yet he spoke like a man who'd done and seen more things than a man twice his age. She rubbed her arms. Looking at him right now, she believed he had.

The sound of Eric's car starting got Trevor's attention. "I guess I'd better be going."

"I guess you'd better." She smiled, then saluted him.

He grinned and shot her one back, then opened the car door...but didn't seem to be in any hurry to get in.

"Oh, Viv's dress!" Christy really wasn't making up excuses for him to stay. Really she wasn't.

Trevor scooped them up and handed them over. "I am—"

"I know. You're formally excused from groveling. You'd better go before Eric implodes."

"Yeah," he said quietly, baby blues piercing like lasers.

Eric backed out and tapped his horn.

Christy glanced over at him, thinking again that he was giving up too easily. Then she realized why.

Dammit. Eric might not know how to get to the lake house, but...

"What's wrong?"

"Eric. He doesn't give up easily. Not when he wants something. And he wants Viv." She debated running in the house and changing and going with Trevor to the reception. But she was the walking dead at this point. Then she eyed Trevor. Hmm. He did owe her one. A giant one. "If you want to repay me for this morning, do me a favor and don't let Kate tell him how to get to the lake house."

"Do you think she'll tell him after everything that's happened?"

Christy just looked at him.

"Right. What was I thinking? I only just met the woman, but I have a feeling Mike's life will never be boring."

Christy more than agreed. "Promise me you won't let him go up there."

"I'll do my best." He climbed in the car, then leaned out the window. "Maybe you should call her anyway. Just in case he finds out from someone else."

There wasn't anyone else who knew—not that Christy was aware of anyway. Viv worked with Christy in ICU and their grueling shift schedule had made it easier to head up to the cabin during the week, making it almost impossible for her other friends to come up. As far she knew, Kate had been the only other one.

"I can't call her," Christy said. "No phones up

there yet. Just cell phones, and the service is spotty at best. She probably turned hers off anyway. But I'll try."

"Okay." But he didn't move. And neither did she.

Eric tapped his horn again and Christy narrowed her gaze at him, knowing his impatience did not stem from a strong desire for wedding cake. He wanted to get to Kate.

"Keep an eye on him."

He merely grinned and gave her a final salute.

Christy was still clutching the sequin dress and robe to her chest when Trevor pulled out. She watched until the car disappeared, then realized she was actually weaving on her feet she was so tired.

It was only when she went up the porch steps that she realized she had no purse. Which meant she also did not have Viv's spare key. And Mr. Military had surely locked the back door.

Perfect. Just perfect. She was too exhausted to work up a good panic. She rooted around the door and porch, but found nothing. Too tired to cry, she simply dumped the dress and shoes on the porch rocker and curled up in the padded porch swing. She'd deal with this much better after she'd had some sleep.

She would have sworn she'd just closed her eyes when someone—gently this time—tried to wake her up.

"Christy, I really hate to do this."

"Then don't," she growled. Her bed was sway-ing. Why was her bed swaying? She was hallucinat-

ing, that was it. It was a dream brought on by an
overload of stress and sleep deprivation. She tried
to snuggle more deeply under her covers...then realized vaguely that there didn't seem to be any
covers. No pillows, either.

"Christy. It's Eric. He's gone. And I don't think
it's to the airport."

On the best of days it took at least three of her six
alarm clocks to wake her up. Right now it would
take an atomic bomb. "Go 'way."

He was shaking her shoulder again. "I know
you're going to kill me for this and I deserve a full
court-martial. I don't know how Eric found out. I
stuck by Kate until she and Mike left for their honeymoon. But one of the bridesmaids said she saw
him leave in a hurry. I'm betting he's headed for the
lake house."

That penetrated the fog. "Wha? Lake house?
Eric?" She sat bolt upright, then groaned and held
her head as the swing rocked. "Someone just shoot
me now."

Then there were strong arms around her and she
simply didn't have it in her to fight.

"Come on. I'm taking you inside."

"Can't. Door's locked." She cracked one eye
open. "And someone didn't let me take my purse
earlier."

"I told you the back door was unlocked."

She wanted to pound on something, namely him,
but her fingers wouldn't make a satisfactory fist. "I
don't even care anymore," she mumbled as he

carted her around back and in through the kitchen door.

The kitchen was a blur, as was the short hallway and the stairs. "Just tell me how to get to the lake house and I'll head up there," he said. "I know Viv doesn't know me, but it might help if she had someone else there."

His words were a velvet buzz in her head.

"Christy, stay with me here. Just long enough to give me directions."

But he laid her on the bed then, and there was softness swallowing her up, so she couldn't concentrate on what he was saying. She did whimper though. "No more triple shifts," she murmured.

"Triple shifts?"

"Can't help it. People keep needing their lives saved," she managed, already burrowing.

The bed dipped as he sat down and she rolled, stopping against the hard, warm length of his thigh.

"You can go," she said. "Fine. I'm fine."

"I need directions."

Directions? Her brain was cotton candy at this point.

"To the lake house."

Then she remembered. Eric. Lake house. "Viv!" She'd shouted the name in her head, but it came out like a croak. She tried to sit up, but he gently pushed her back down.

"You're not going anywhere but to sleep. As soon as you give me directions."

She sighed and lay back, her eyes felt like they

were filled with sand so she kept them shut. "Take 64 west to 81, then south to 317. It's about fifteen miles straight up the mountain. There's a sign. It's the next dirt road on your left after that. You'll see the house. Log cabin, big screened porch." She swore under her breath. She really should go with him. She tried to sit up again. "Just let me get dressed."

"Absolutely not." He pressed her down again. "If you don't get some sleep, you'll make yourself sick. I wouldn't have come back at all, but I thought you'd want me to do something."

He smoothed the hair from her face, the feel of his blunt-tipped fingers on her skin made her shiver in pleasure. If he'd just keep stroking her skin like that, she could die a happy woman. "Thank you. For going."

"It's the least I could do, considering."

She wanted to say she could think of a whole lot more things he could be doing, but none of them had anything to do with Vivian and Eric. She frowned. Just thinking about Eric barging in up there and invading Vivian's one sanctuary. Not that Viv had ever really worried about Eric intruding anywhere else. He'd been living in Stockholm for the past eighteen months.

"I want to go," Christy said, trying to marshal her wits. "I should be there. This is all my fault."

"I don't see how that is." He kept up his insidious hair stroking. The room was swimming.

"I can sleep in the car." Right at that moment, she

was fairly certain she could have slept while parachuting from a plane.

"I'll handle it."

"She'll want me there. I want to be there." She harnessed all her energy and pushed his hand away, then clawed her way to a sitting position. "I'm going."

Trevor just sighed. "Why did I leave the service again?"

She smiled wearily. "Because you missed the moment-to-moment excitement of the real world?"

"That must be it."

She swung her feet over the side of the bed. "I'm ready."

"I can see that." He had to prop her upright to keep her from sinking backward. "Did you pack some clothes when you came here?"

She nodded. "Duffel. By the closet."

"Purse?"

"Downstairs, next to the phone."

With a bracing hand on her shoulder to keep her upright, he stood and lifted her into his arms.

"You really have to stop doing this."

He looked down into her eyes. "Actually, I'm finding I enjoy carting you around."

Christy managed to bat her eyelashes. "Oh, Commander, you'll turn a girl's head, talking about her like she's a sack of potatoes."

He grinned. "That's me. Mr. Romantic."

Christy could have told him that he had Mr. Sexual Tension down pat just with the eye stare, but it would have gone straight to his head. Besides, she wasn't up to sexual banter, or anything else sexual, either. "Put me down."

"Uh-uh. The deal is, I'm carrying you, a blanket and all of those pillows to the car, where you will make a nest in the back seat and promise not to move or speak until we arrive at the lake."

She managed a salute. "Unless I'm talking or tossing in my sleep, that won't be a concern, sir, Commander, sir."

"Very funny."

"Yeah, that's me. A laugh riot."

His smile faded. "Maybe—"

"Maybe you should get my duffel bag."

"Yeah. Maybe I should." But he wasn't moving. He was looking at her. And not moving. Just looking.

Her pulse bumped a notch, maybe two or three notches. Was he really lowering his head? Was he going to—? Did she want him to? Then his lips brushed her forehead and her heart sank to her stomach. Apparently the answer was yes, she did want him to. Almost desperately. And not on the forehead. She wanted to feel his mouth on hers. "Trevor?"

"Hmm?"

Velvet voice. That's what he was. Mr. Velvet Voice.

"We'd better go." *Before I do something foolish, like beg you to kiss me.*

"Yeah. Close your eyes."

"What?"

"Relax. Sleep. I'll wake you up when we get there. Or try to anyway," he added with a grin.

"So I'm a heavy sleeper," she said, but she let her eyes drift shut and pressed her face to his chest as he carried her down the stairs. "Sue me." He even smelled good. Really good.

"There's a lot of things you make me want to do," she thought she heard him murmur. "Not one of them litigious."

But the beat of his heart was lulling her back to dreamland. And she liked dreamland. She liked it a lot. In dreamland, he didn't kiss her on the forehead.

5

As HE BOUNCED over the rutted lanes, Trevor wished he'd rented a Jeep instead of a sedan. He also wished he'd changed out of his uniform into something a lot less constrictive. Part of that particular problem had to do with the woman presently crashed out in his back seat.

He wasn't sure he'd ever remained in such a constant state of semiarousal around a woman. Even now, just thinking about her... He glanced in the rearview mirror. Something he'd done more often than necessary during the three-hour drive.

She'd been out cold before he'd pulled out of the driveway and had stayed that way since. And he still couldn't keep his eyes, or his thoughts, off her. He'd been on a plane less than twenty-four hours ago, heading to a wedding, and to the start of a new life for himself.

He looked back at the road just in time to hit a rather large ditch. He winced and darted a quick look over his shoulder before maneuvering around another giant hole. Christy grumbled a little, but otherwise didn't so much as budge. He still couldn't believe he'd found her sleeping on the porch swing when he'd come back to Viv's place. He'd hated having to wake her up again, but Kate and Mike had left the reception, and by the time he'd figured out where Eric had disappeared to, there wasn't anyone left to give him directions to the lake. He wasn't even sure Eric was up there, but he figured Christy would want to know anyway.

And yet he couldn't honestly say he minded being the one to tell her. It gave him a reason to see her again. He didn't really know her at all, yet he'd been with her in circumstances that were somewhat intimate and personal. He knew if he walked away now, she'd stick in his mind and it had been a long time since a woman had stuck in his mind. But then, he'd worked hard to keep that from happening. His career hadn't been conducive to long-term, or even short-term relationships.

And he'd long since tired of brief liaisons. Just as he'd tired of dragging himself all over the world to solve problems his government would just as soon pretend it didn't have. The world was evolving, more countries were becoming democracies and developing their own local law-enforcement agencies that operated separately from their military troops, and they were looking to the U.S. to find a way to develop that kind of criminal justice system. He still wanted to serve his country, but as a civilian, in charge of his own operation, training cops and former military personnel to go over to these countries and help them begin the arduous task of setting up local law enforcement.

He also wanted the stability of staying in one place. He was ready for that. So he'd come home. Or at least to the one place that had ever felt like home. But he hadn't thought much beyond that. Hadn't thought about a social life, or even if he wanted to work on having one. He had a business to build, although he'd begun setting it up well in advance of his discharge.

He looked in the mirror again. He certainly hadn't planned on her.

Just then the log cabin came into view. He could see the lake several hundred feet beyond it. It was a gorgeous setting, peaceful and remote. He'd spent most of the last ten years in remote spots, but rarely beautiful. He'd wanted the bustle and noise and civility of a city, which was another reason he'd chosen Richmond. But maybe, just maybe, an escape like this would be welcome from time to time. Maybe he was the one who was sleep deprived. How else could he explain the odd thoughts he was having? Thoughts about what it would be like to head away for a private weekend to a cabin like this...with a woman like Christy.

But they weren't alone. And this wasn't any romantic getaway. And other than the fact that she slept like the dead and was fiercely protective of her friends, he didn't really know what kind of woman Christy was. But he wanted to be alone with her. He wanted to find out what kind of woman she was.

He pulled into the short gravel drive next to the

house. A small red import was parked close to the side walkway. Eric's blue rental was just behind it.

Trevor swore under his breath. The only getaway that was going to happen was getting Eric away from Vivian. Hopefully as peacefully as possible.

He shut off the engine and looked over his shoulder. Christy needed far more than three hours of sleep. What drove her to work herself into the ground like that, anyway?

People keep needing their lives saved.

He recalled her words and realized he understood that particular drive, maybe better than most. He opened his door carefully, quietly, although he probably could have set off the alarm without disturbing her. She'd be fine right where she was, he decided. For now anyway.

He turned toward the house. Well, at least there was no screaming or sounds of breaking dishware. He walked up the side pathway and headed to the front door. What would he say? Why was he here, butting into the lives of two people he didn't even know? A crying bride, that's why. He was never going near another one. Ever.

"How did you get up here?"

Trevor turned and spied Vivian, or at least the woman he assumed was Vivian, walking up from the shoreline of the lake. But she wasn't talking to him. She hadn't seen him yet. Her question was addressed to Eric, who was striding toward her. Apparently he'd just gotten here himself.

"Why didn't you come to the wedding?" Eric responded. "I can't believe you left Kate high and dry like that. It's not like you."

Vivian stopped and folded her arms.

Trevor winced. *Not a good opener, my friend.*

"You don't have any idea whether it's like me or not," she said. "You only know the me you wanted me to be. Well, surprise, surprise." She spread her arms wide. "This is who I am. A woman who doesn't take kindly to other people messing with her life."

Eric's steps faltered then, as if he'd never encountered this particular attitude before.

Trevor silently applauded Vivian. And wished he'd never come up here. This was private, between the two of them. He thought about trying to silently retrace his steps, but just then Vivian spied him.

He swore inwardly, but smiled and waved. "Hello, I'm Trevor McQuillen, a friend of Mike's."

"Oh, great. So Kate's got him involved in this, too. That's just lovely. Were you the one who brought him up here?"

This is going well, he thought ruefully. But what had he expected? "No. Actually, I was trying to prevent him from coming up here."

"Well, bless Mike then. At least he has a brain in his head."

Trevor cleared his throat. "Actually, you have Christy to thank for that."

"Vivian—" Eric began.

But Vivian ignored him. "Christy? What in the world does she have to do with this?"

"I—it's a long story." He really didn't want to be here.

Eric stepped in then. "I just want a chance to talk with you." He looked at Trevor. "Alone."

Trevor would have liked nothing better than to give Eric what he wanted, but he looked to Vivian to decide. It was her property and her life being invaded.

She looked between the two of them, then sighed. "Okay, talk. But he stays."

Eric's eyes widened, but this time he wisely capitulated. "Fine, fine. But can we at least have some privacy?"

Vivian looked uncertainly at Trevor and once again, he took command of a situation he should never have been involved in to begin with. He smiled and motioned to the lakeshore. "Why don't you two stay here and talk? If you don't mind, I'd like to change clothes."

Vivian nodded, then stiffened her resolve and looked to Eric. "You have until he gets back out here, so start talking."

"Vivian—"

"Clock is ticking."

Trevor hid his smile as he crossed back toward the car. He'd wondered at the wisdom of leaving the two of them so close to a body of water. But if anyone's life was in danger it was Eric's. He was going to have to take care of himself, although apparently that was what he excelled at anyway.

And Trevor should know. He'd been taking care of himself for longer than he could remember.

He gently popped the trunk and took out the duffel he'd carried off the plane. The rest of his stuff had been shipped ahead and was in storage. He didn't even have a place to stay yet. Mike had offered his place while they were out of town on their honeymoon, but Trevor had booked a suite in a residential hotel.

He'd spent what little leave he'd had setting up his business, leasing the property and revamping the buildings that had been on it to suit his needs. He could always bunk there if he couldn't locate something right away. After all, he'd probably be spending most of his time there anyway.

He checked in on Christy, guilt creeping in again as he saw how cramped and curled up she was in order to fit her not-so-petite frame on the back seat. He wondered if he could carry her into the house without waking her up.

He looked back to the lake. Vivian was still holding herself at a distance from her ex, who was gesturing wildly as he paced back and forth. From the look of things, Trevor could have left Christy sleeping on the porch swing. He didn't think Eric's visit was going to last too long.

Well, they were all up here now and the sun was setting. Likely they'd all end up here for the night. Unless Eric continued to make an ass out of himself. Trevor had stuck his nose in this far, he might as well stick it in the rest of the way. If Viv wasn't comfortable having Eric in her home, Trevor would see to it that he wasn't.

He swung his duffel over his shoulder and headed for the screened-in porch, deciding to scope out the cabin before trying to bring Christy inside. Another glance at the lake had him smiling. Now it was Vivian gesturing and pacing. Well, at least they were both talking. He wondered if either of them were listening.

None of your business, McQuillen. Besides, what he knew about marriage, successful or otherwise, could fit on the business end of a bullet.

The inside of the cabin was spacious and comfortably furnished, with the decor on the homey side. There were green-and-yellow plaid curtains on the windows, matching the pale green-and-lemon-yellow covers on the two couches. There were numerous brightly colored chairs and throw pillows, all muted by the exposed log walls and fronted by a huge picture window with a view of the lake and pier. The other end of the room boasted a heavy stone mantle over a large fireplace.

The air up here was decidedly less humid, and now that the sun was setting, decidedly cooler, too. Maybe they'd have a fire later. He could bring Christy in and let her nest on the couch that faced the fireplace.

He smiled and shook his head. "You're not here to play house any more than you're here to play marriage counselor." He headed off in search of the bathroom, thinking the sooner he got off this mountain, out of these people's lives and back to business, the better.

He emerged from the cabin ten minutes later to the rumbling sound of thunder. "Wonderful," he muttered, looking up through the towering pines that sheltered the cabin to the rapidly darkening sky. Unless Eric was booted out shortly, no one would be going anywhere once the skies opened up.

"What have I done to deserve this? I eat my vegetables, pay my taxes on time and even help little old ladies across the street." Or he would have if there had been any in the parts of the world he'd inhabited of late.

Maybe that was his problem. He'd been so busy trying to do his part to make the world a safer place that he'd totally lost track of what the world was really like.

He looked over at Viv and Eric. Neither was gesturing or pacing at this point. In fact, they were sitting at opposite ends of a picnic table and talking. *Really* talking from the looks of things. He looked at his car, where Christy was still dead to the world in the back seat.

Maybe this *was* the real world. Maybe there was no such thing as boring, routine lives. Maybe no matter where he went, life would be messy, complicated, unpredictable. Not so different really, from what he'd left behind.

Except that it was *his* life now.

A thumping noise dragged him from his thoughts.

A swirl of blanket, a smashed pillow, followed by a nest of dark hair, rose from the back seat. A hand reached out blindly, clawing at the blanket and hair, finally revealing a face still puffy and wrinkled with sleep. She blinked several times, then yawned ferociously and stretched.

Trevor's heart banged once against his chest. Hard. She did that to him. Even looking like the Creature from the Black Lagoon she did that to him. Made his heart bang.

And rather than run screaming off the mountain, back to some other version of the real world that had to be out there somewhere, he was smiling, crossing to the car and actually looking forward to whatever sleepy, grumbling thing she had to say. Because it meant she was awake, and that he was still in her crazy world.

"You locked me in here," she said through the glass. "First you lock me out of my house, then you lock me in your car. What kind of person are you anyway?"

A person who has obviously lost his mind, he thought.

He pressed the button on his key ring and popped the locks. "First of all, I didn't lock you out of your house. The back door was unlocked. And I didn't lock you in my car, I locked other people out. You can open the door with that button right there," he said, pointing to the black button marked Lock. He grinned at her when she scowled at him. "Have a nice rest?"

She kicked at the blanket and blew her hair from her face. "Except for the seat belt permanently embedded into my lower back, oh yeah, felt like I was on a cloud." She scooted to the edge of the seat. "How long have we been here? Did you talk to Vivian? What's going on?"

He tugged her duffel from the front seat, took the blanket from her and traded it for her bag. "Why don't you go inside and take a shower and change into your own clothes? You'll feel better."

She smiled then, making the sleep lines on her face crinkle. "Are you saying I don't wake up gorgeous and perky?"

He could have told her the truth, that sleep wrinkles, rat's nest hair and all, she still made his heart bang. But that would be a tactical error. And Lord knew he'd had already more of those in one day than he had in his entire career in special ops. Thank goodness the only life at stake today was his own.

"I'm saying you'll probably feel better in your own clothes. Shower is, of course, optional."

She considered him then and he realized he'd left himself wide open, but she apparently decided to withdraw her forces and leave the good fight for another time. He was almost disappointed.

The thunder rolled again and she frowned. He didn't miss the light shiver, either. It was cooler here, but far from cold. "Not a fan of thunderstorms?"

She didn't even try to pretend otherwise. "Very not a fan." This time a split of lightning lit the sky through the trees and she hustled to the front door with a good deal more energy than he'd have given her credit for being able to muster. She glanced down to the lake as she stepped into the porch and spied Viv and Eric. She paused, then another rumbler had her scooting inside and slapping the door shut. "Tell Viv I'll be out in a few minutes. I can't believe you didn't wake me up!"

Then she was gone. Which was good, because then she wouldn't get mad at him for laughing. "Wake her up, she says." *Sure, me and my brass marching band.* Apparently thunder worked wonders, though. He wondered if they made an alarm clock that sounded like a storm brewing.

Viv came striding up from the lake, Eric following behind at a slower, more thoughtful pace.

"Was that Christy?"

Trevor nodded.

"Why didn't you tell me she was with you?"

Trevor remained calm in the face of her irritation. She looked battle weary and with good reason. "She was asleep, and you were talking to Eric."

"Well...fine," she said, blowing out a deep sigh and most of her frustration along with it. "I'm sorry. It's just..." She tried to smile. "Saying 'It's been a long day' doesn't seem to do this one justice."

Trevor smiled. "Yes, ma'am."

Vivian was a slight woman with spiky, strawberry hair, pale-blue eyes and freckles splashed across her cheeks. Her smile came easily enough, but the weariness in her eyes cast a shadow over it.

"Looks like we're in for a boomer. It's coming in off the lake, which always means a loud one." She nodded to the door. "We should all get inside."

"Christy made a beeline when she heard the first one," he said, holding the door open for her, looking back for Eric, but he was walking over to his car.

"She's not a fan of storms," was all Viv said, but he sensed there was more to that story.

"Is Eric going to try and leave with this storm coming up?" he asked.

She opened the door and held it for him, looking past him at Eric and shook her head. He couldn't tell if she was unhappy about this...or merely resigned to what fate had dumped on her. Fate and a certain newly wedded best friend.

"He's just getting his bag. None of us are going anywhere tonight. The road down the mountain will be one giant river five minutes after this storm busts open. If it blows through quickly, it will be muddy and boggy tomorrow, but passable as soon as the wind and sun have at it for a few hours." She closed the door behind him. "I guess now's as good a time as any for you to tell me who the hell you are and how you came to have Christy sleeping in your car." She perched on a stool at the bar that separated the kitchen from the dining area and, smiling, propped her chin on her hands. "Apparently, I've got all night."

Trevor liked her. She was a battler and she had spirit. He took the stool next to her. "Okay. But only if you tell me why your friend is afraid of storms."

"Why don't you ask her yourself?"

He grinned. "Because you probably won't hurt me."

She grinned, her curiosity apparent. "You know Christy pretty well."

"Not really. I only met her today." Trevor leaned on the counter. "But I want to get to know her better."

Vivian raised her eyebrows, but her dark eyes danced. "Well, well. I'd warn you that you're competing against an entire hospital filled with people who need her." She folded her arms across her chest and studied him openly. "But somehow I don't think you're going to let that stand in your way."

"No, ma'am," he said with a smile. But Trevor really had no idea what in the hell he was doing, much less what his plans were. He heard the shower start up, pictured Christy climbing out of that choir gown, and realized he'd never wanted a shower so badly in his life.

So what exactly *was* he planning?

The storm was building. Christy was naked not fifty feet away. Vivian was staring at him expectantly, and any second her ex-husband was going to come walking through the cabin door in God knows what kind of emotional state. And Trevor was going to be trapped in this cabin with all three of them. All night.

Again he wondered how in the hell he'd ended up here.

And why he wasn't all that upset about it.

6

CHRISTY GROANED with almost orgasmic pleasure as the water beat down on her back. She wanted to go back to sleep, but no way was that going to happen during the storm. She realized now what had woken her up. She shuddered under the pelting hot water, tempted to stay right where she was until the thunderstorm passed. If she kept the water running hard enough, she might not even hear it.

As if the gods of thunder had heard her—and laughed—the walls shook with another rocking blast. Deciding there were smarter places to be other than standing in water during an electrical storm, she shut the water off and reluctantly got out.

Of course, she now had to face the storm, *and* Trevor, Vivian and Eric. Maybe standing in water and wishing for a lightning bolt was the better alternative.

Then she smelled the elixir of life and groaned, heavily undecided. Vivian's dad had his own special blend of coffee he claimed was mixed by the fairies of his homeland. Of course, it might have been the whiskey he added to it. She didn't care. Right now a shot of both would do her good. It was almost worth braving the storm or all three of the people on the other side of the door. But both together...

"Well, maybe the storm inside the cabin will take my mind off the storm outside the cabin."

She quickly dressed in baggy shorts and a sweatshirt, telling herself she didn't care what Trevor thought of how she looked. She hadn't exactly packed her bombshell clothes for a weekend at Viv's. Not that she even had bombshell clothes. She was fairly certain there was more to being a bombshell than a little black dress, anyway. "Or a fruit-salad sequin one for that matter." She groaned even as she laughed. He'd already seen her doing her bombshell routine. Boobshell was more like it, she thought. Of course, prior to that fiasco, he'd seen her in pretty much nothing at all.

What did she care anyway, right? She was above all that, above worrying about appearances. It was all about the inner woman these days. And she was nothing if not a confident woman of the new millennium. Right?

Then she made the mistake of looking in the mirror. Her cheeks were overly flushed, her hair stuck to her head and her eyelids were still puffy. "Oh, yeah, you're the new-millennium goddess."

Well, Trevor had better embrace her inner woman, because the outer woman was enough to scare off Frankenstein. She stopped with her hand on the doorknob. Wait, she didn't want Trevor embracing anything. Did she?

He was too controlling, too overwhelming...too damn sexy. She sighed and leaned her forehead against the door. Okay, something was really wrong with her. Too damn sexy was supposed to be a good thing. With Lieutenant Commander Trevor Mc-Quillen it was a downright hormone grabber. So what was her problem?

Gorgeous men didn't usually have the hots for her, that's what. She was a bit too tall, a bit too broad of shoulder and hip. She snorted. And maybe a teensy bit opinionated and self-confident. So what?

So she was more the starving-artist or boring office-manager type. Military men, gorgeous, commanding military men...nope. Never had attracted them.

But Trevor had looked into her eyes, touched her face and told her he wanted to get to know her better. She sighed and traced a finger over her cheek. Of course, she thought, her boobs had been spilling out in his face at the time. He might have simply been in a hormonal, breast-induced fog. She'd run into men like that.

And then there was that kiss. He'd kissed her on the forehead like a brother, or best friend. Yep, that would be her luck. He'd think of her like a sister. Or worse. A pal. She'd run into men like that, too. Too many of them. And most of them were still her friends. Big sister to the world, that was her.

She gripped the doorknob again. She didn't want to be Trevor's big sister, or his pal. She wasn't sure what she did want to be, either, but one way or the other, he was going to sit up and take notice of her. Whatever happened, she'd be damned if he would end up thinking of her as simply "a good friend."

She flipped her wet hair back, straightened her perfectly fine shoulders and flung open the door. Her grand entrance was totally ruined by the biggest bolt of lightning she'd ever witnessed. She jumped and squealed, drawing the immediate attention of everyone in the room.

Lovely. Femme fatales didn't squeal. She was pretty sure it was on the first page of their handbook.

She peeled off the hand she'd plastered to her chest and tried to laugh and look totally unaffected by the fact that she could have been killed where she stood. It was much harder than it might seem, since she knew firsthand that lightning bolts did indeed kill people. One had killed her best friend when she was nine. She'd dealt with the death and the grisly misfortune of having witnessed it. But she'd never been able to get past her fear of electrical storms.

Trevor was off his stool and halfway across the room, his eyes filled with a look that told her he understood. Far too much.

She turned on Viv. "You told him?"

Vivian managed to look guiltless except for the tiny spots of color that bloomed on her pale, freckled cheeks. It was the curse of the Irish, she'd always said, and one she hated. But right now Christy wasn't feeling so sorry for her.

"He asked," Viv said with a little shrug.

"Oh, well, fine then. Silly me," she said, turning to Trevor. "Anything else you want to know? Apparently my life is an open book."

"Don't be mad at Viv. I knew you were upset earlier and it didn't seem like you, so I was curious."

Christy was curious, too. "It didn't *seem* like me? You don't even know me."

Trevor grinned. "I'm working on that."

Christy felt the power of that grin all the way down to her toes. Well. So. She took a breath and tried to corral her inner-millennium woman strength. "If you want to know something, just ask me, okay?"

"He figured he'd end up less injured by going through me," Viv said with a cheeky smile. "He knows you better than you think."

"Oh, very funny. You two are a regular laugh riot. Maybe I should go back in the bathroom so you guys can continue having fun at my expense."

"Oh, no, it's much more fun teasing you to your face."

"Your turn will come," Christy warned.

"It's always my turn," Viv said, laughing. "Coffee is ready. I went light on the coffee for you in deference to the current weather situation."

"Bless you, all is forgiven," Christy said, taking the foamy mug Viv handed her. She looked around but didn't see Eric. "Where is the fourth in this little drama?"

Viv's smile immediately vanished and Christy

wished the question back, but as usual her mouth had operated before her brain.

"He's in the other bathroom."

Christy put a hand on her friend's arm. "You okay? I'm really sorry. We tried to stop him."

A spark returned to Viv's pale eyes. "So I heard. I bet you looked better in that dress than I ever did."

"Honey, no one could make that dress look good."

They both laughed, but it died quickly when the master bedroom door opened and Eric stepped out. He tried to smile, but the tension fairly screamed off him. "I certainly know how to make an entrance, don't I?"

Vivian's eyes shuttered and she turned away. Christy wasn't sure what had passed between them so far, but obviously nothing too wonderful. Not that she was surprised. She shot Eric a look as Vivian retreated to the kitchen on the other side of the bar, but he only had eyes for his ex-wife.

"I think I have the makings for spaghetti," Vivian said to the group at large. "Christy, can you toss the salad?" A small smile came back to her then. "It's not technically cooking, so you shouldn't screw it up too badly."

Christy made a face at her, but was glad to see her friend braving her way through this. She'd dealt with a lot these past eighteen months and was a much stronger woman for it. But she had to be on an emotional roller coaster right now and Christy felt helpless.

"I'll make the salad," Eric offered quietly, coming to the other side of the bar. "I always liked your spaghetti."

Christy immediately opened her mouth to override his offer, but a quick look from Viv had her closing it again.

Well, what do you know? Maybe more had happened than she'd thought.

"Okay. The greens are in the bottom drawer of the fridge," Viv told him.

He moved into the small kitchen, careful not to brush against Viv, Christy noted with approval. Eric was still Eric, which she was forced to recall wasn't all bad, and it actually looked like he was trying.

Viv slid the cutting block and a few tomatoes toward him, along with a knife. "Here, you can chop these."

Eric smiled and this time Christy saw the boyish light in his eyes that used to always be there whenever he looked at his wife. She wondered what Viv saw when she looked into his eyes.

"You sure you wouldn't rather keep the sharp blades close by?" he asked.

Viv actually laughed. "My tongue is sharp enough, don't you think?"

Smiling, Eric looked to Trevor. "Any expert military advice on how best to answer that one?"

He held his hands up. "You're asking the wrong strategist. I could get you out of Bosnia in one piece, but I wouldn't make any bets on getting you out of that kitchen in the same condition."

Everyone laughed and Christy saw Viv's shoulders relax a little as she went about browning the meat on the stove. Maybe this evening wouldn't be so horrible after all. If they could all be civil, she'd be thankful enough.

Thunder shook the house again and a torrent of rain began pelting the huge picture windows.

Trevor was beside Christy before she could think to attempt to mask her automatic reaction. "Hey, you want to play cards, checkers? Something to take your mind off things?"

His voice was so deep, so vibrant, it caused a storm all its own inside her. Several things he could do to distract her came to mind. None of them board games. "Nothing will take my mind off of it. Except perhaps three or four more of these," she added, sipping at her Irish coffee again. "Then I'd be too sick to care."

"I'm sorry about your friend," he said quietly, holding her gaze.

"It was a long time ago."

"Time doesn't heal every wound."

She gave him a considering look. "You sound like you're speaking from personal experience."

He didn't say anything, but he didn't have to. He'd obviously dealt with some unpleasant things in his life, too.

"It's a silly fear," she said, curious about just what those things were. Even though it was none of her business. "I've even seen a counselor friend of mine at the hospital about it." She shrugged. "We both understand where it comes from, and I totally real-ize the chances of it happening again are pretty much nil." She laughed lightly. "I mean, I'm a nurse, for God's sake. We don't see many lightning victims, you know?" She shrugged. "But I don't seem to be able to get past it." Lightning lit up the outside, followed by a loud cracking boom that made her jump. She laughed nervously. "See? My rational brain knows not to be afraid, but my body freaks every time. It's so stupid."

He took her hand and tugged her closer. "Not so stupid."

"It is. I'm a grown woman," she said, suddenly more nervous about the electrical storm in his blue eyes than the one raging outside.

"So I've noticed."

"I, um... Well."

He grinned. "I've done it. I've rendered her speechless."

She found a smile of her own. "I think I've been pretty quiet around you for most of the time we've spent together."

"Only because you were unconscious. And even then..."

She raised her eyebrows when he let the sentence dangle. "Are you insinuating I snore?"

"I wouldn't call it snoring. In the strictest sense of the word, anyway. More like...snuffling."

"Oh, well, gee. I feel ever so much better now, thanks. I don't snore. I snuffle. Me and the ele-phants."

Trevor laughed. "I'm making such a good first impression here, aren't I?"

"And second and third." But she was laughing, too. And he was making a great second and third impression. In fact, she realized she was actually enjoying herself. Storm, divorced couple and all. "Must be the military training. If at first you don't succeed, and all that."

His eyes all but glowed in the dimming light. "I always succeed. Eventually."

Christy swallowed, and when her throat proved too dry for that, she took a gulp of coffee...then choked when the whiskey hit the back of her throat.

Trevor thumped her on the back and took her mug away so she wouldn't slosh it all over the place. "You okay?"

No, she wasn't remotely okay. Not because of the whiskey, but because she'd realized something. Something she'd only really started to come to terms with in the bathroom. She wanted Trevor McQuillen. Bad. And unless she was totally mistaken, the feeling was mutual. All she had to do was not screw things up.

Oh, great. Her batting average wasn't that good.

The rafters shook overhead and she shook right along with them. Only, for once, her mind wasn't on the storm.

"Christy?"

She snapped her gaze up to his. "What? Oh, I'm fine. Fine." Now what did she do? Bat her eyelashes at him? Jump him?

Think, think. What did she normally do when a guy made it clear he wanted her? Well, let's see. Um. As it turned out, she had no data stored for that particular possibility. Normally a guy just said, "Hey, you wanna go out?" and she either said yes or pretended she didn't hear him.

So did she just wait for Trevor to ask her out?

Somehow that didn't seem the millennium-woman way to handle this. She'd always been bold and confident in all the other areas of her life, mainly because she was pretty confident about the other areas of her life. But when it came to dealing with the opposite sex, where relationships were concerned...well, everyone had to have an Achilles' heel, right?

But she'd certainly been bold and confident with him up to this point, so it didn't seem right to back down and play the waiting game now. Especially since she didn't want to wait. In fact, if it weren't for Viv and Eric...

"Where are you?"

She blinked at him. "I'm pretty sure I'm right here, why?"

"You're standing here, but your thoughts are a million miles away."

No they weren't, she could have told him. They were right here, about six inches in front of her. Right where he stood, deep inside her usual personal-space comfort zone. And yet those six inches might as well have been the Grand Canyon for all that she knew how to close them. With the exception of throwing herself at him—literally—and that didn't seem prudent with an audience in the kitchen.

She glanced over and saw Viv and Eric working in silence, but totally oblivious to her and Trevor. She supposed that was a good thing.

"Do you think they'll work things out?" Trevor asked quietly.

"I'm not so sure trying to do that is the best thing for Viv. I know Eric wants to, and I'll even give him the fact that it looks like he's trying, but..." She shrugged and took her mug back from him. "I just don't want to see her ever go through that kind of pain again."

"Sometimes you have to risk the pain to get the glory."

She looked at him. "I'm not so sure how glorious marriage is, when you get right down to it."

He looked surprised at her summation. "No good-marriage role models in your life?"

"One or two, I guess, but even with them it seems like such a high-risk gamble, you know?"

"What about your folks?"

"My mom and dad were pretty happy. I don't remember my dad all that much—he died when I was little."

"I'm sorry. Losing two people early on like that couldn't have been easy."

She was confused for a moment, then remembered he knew about her childhood friend. "Well, my dad was sick pretty much from the time I was born, so we were prepared for that. As much as you can be anyway."

"So your mom didn't remarry?"

"Oh, sure, several times." She smiled then. "But you'd have to meet my mom to understand that I don't expect her to be a role model where marriage is concerned." No, Ruby Russell was an entity unto herself. "Maybe if my dad had been healthy and had lived she'd have been more...traditional." Then she laughed outright. "No, scratch that. She might have stayed married to my dad, but she could never be accused of being conventional."

"Sounds like an interesting woman."

"That and more—trust me." Which was why Christy was ever thankful that her mom had moved to Palm Beach with husband number three several years back and stayed down there after he'd passed on. It was harder to meddle in her daughter's love life long distance. Not impossible, but harder. "But she's a big believer in marriage. She just hasn't perfected the art herself."

"So is that why you don't think it's a glorious thing? Too high a risk to find out if you can 'perfect the art,' as it were?"

She grinned. "Just how did we get on this subject anyway? I feel like I've spilled half my life story in five minutes."

"I told you I planned to get to know you better."

Charmed and dangerous. She'd been right about that. "Well, now it's your five minutes. Are you the gung-ho type that believes every couple should stay together no matter what?"

"Not at all. But if there was something there worth having initially and the two people involved can't seem to move on past it, then maybe it's not over yet."

She cocked her head. "Speaking from personal experience?"

"Not me. Never married, never tempted."

"Then who were you referring to? Don't tell me Viv and Eric. This comes from some other place. You were too adamant."

He grinned. "You're no slouch in interrogation techniques, either, you know."

She batted her lashes. "Who, me? I'm just asking innocent questions here."

"You, innocent? Right."

"I think I'm insulted."

"Don't be. Sharp and on the ball are far more interesting then naive and empty-headed."

She sipped her drink, trying to swallow his directness at the same time. "You give great compliments."

"I say what I mean."

She looked at him over the rim of her cup. "Don't sidetrack me. Who were you referring to earlier? Your parents?"

"I was actually talking about my grandmother. She raised me. At least the early years. Or she tried to."

"Meaning?"

"I was...a handful as they say."

She widened her eyes in mock surprise. "You? I'm shocked."

"You don't even know me," he said laughing.

And then the millennium woman finally burst forth. She lowered her mug and smiled at him. "Well, things can change, can't they?"

7

TREVOR LOOKED into Christy's dark eyes and wondered where she'd been all his life. Smart, funny, sharp, direct. And just vulnerable enough to appeal to his he-man protect-his-woman side. He hid a grin. Oh, she'd have a field day with him if he ever let that little thought slip out. "I think things are already changing," he said, reaching up to toy with the damp ringlets of hair that were going in all different directions as they dried.

"Dinner's ready," Viv announced.

Christy jumped as if thunder had rocked them both. And just maybe it had.

"Thank you," she said to him as they headed to the dining nook.

"For?"

She smiled up at him. "I forgot about the storm for a while."

He grinned and pulled out a chair for her. "Anytime."

She looked up at him as she took her seat. "Be careful what you offer. You'll get a phone call at three in the morning from a hysterical woman begging to be distracted."

His entire body leaped in reaction, though he realized she hadn't meant it to sound so provocative. Which just made it all the more so. He leaned down by her ear as he helped push her chair in. "Promise? I'll make sure to give you my home, cell and pager numbers before we leave."

He felt her shiver and it was all he could do not to touch her. God, he ached to kiss that smart mouth of hers.

"Sit down," she hissed under her breath.

He grinned. So, she could be gotten to after all. In fact, when he thought about it, the only time she seemed at a loss was when he made it clear he wanted her. Although she was finding her feet there, as well. He pulled up his chair, catty-corner to her, and tried to decide if he wanted to let her find them...or sweep her off of them.

"Salad?" Viv offered, passing the large wooden bowl to him and snapping him from his thoughts.

"Thanks." He looked in the bowl, then to Eric's hands.

"What?" Eric said, looking at his hands, as well.

"Just making sure nothing else got lopped into the salad."

Eric laughed. "If she'd wanted to lop something off, it wouldn't be my fingers."

Trevor winced and both Viv and Christy burst out laughing.

"No," Viv said, still laughing. "His fingers were never a problem. In fact—" She broke off, her bravado giving way to a blush.

Eric smiled, but wisely turned his attention to his salad and didn't comment.

Trevor watched Christy watching the exchange and knew she was wondering just what had gone on beneath the surface in that silent kitchen. Even though he didn't know the couple, he was undeniably curious, as well. Human nature, he supposed. But Eric looked to be trying and Viv wasn't giving off any hostile signals. Quite the opposite actually.

"Heavy thinking with your salad?" Trevor said quietly as he passed her the dressing.

She glanced over at him, seemingly surprised by the comment. Did she think she was that hard to read? Or maybe she just wasn't used to anyone paying close attention. He couldn't seem to not pay her close attention. He smiled when he realized her thoughts had drifted again. He waggled the bottle of dressing in front of her and she laughed and blushed at the same time.

"Wandering thoughts," she said, taking the bottle from him.

"Tell me more."

"Hey, what are you two whispering about over there?" Viv demanded good-naturedly. "Miss Russell, if you have something to say, why don't you share it with the whole class?"

Christy smirked and tossed a crouton at her.

Viv batted it away. "No food fights in this cafeteria or you'll go straight to the principal's office."

Christy darted a look at Trevor and he had to swallow his grin. She had this sort of...sinful look on her face. As if she'd been imagining being sent to him... For what he was dying to know. He merely held her gaze, as if to say "Anyplace, anytime."

He observed the tiniest little shiver race over her and his body stirred. Oh, to be alone with her right now. Her gaze flickered to his hands and his body hardened. So...he thought, trying not to clutch his wineglass any tighter or the stem would break. Did she want his hands on her? Because he'd be more than willing to accommodate that desire.

"Earth to Christy."

She snapped her attention to Viv, the most becoming blush staining her cheeks. "Can't a girl eat without all these interruptions?" she muttered. "It's not often I get noncafeteria food."

"Or nonnuked food," Viv added. She looked to Trevor. "If she ever offers to cook dinner for you, here's a hint. Order in."

Christy raised her fork. "Guilty as charged. If God had wanted me to cook, he wouldn't have invented microwaves and Lean Cuisine."

"I can cook," Trevor assured her, his gaze firmly on Christy however, who was making a close study of her plate.

Viv beamed. "Good, then you can handle breakfast detail."

"Yes, ma'am," he responded, then lifted his wineglass in a toast. "Good meal, Vivian. And Eric. Thank you for the hospitality." He all but felt Christy relax beside him as the topic and focus shifted away from her. Well, she didn't know it, but his focus was not so easily swayed.

"Storm looks like it's blowing over," Eric said as they all finished up.

"Still raining, though," Viv added. "The road down will be a mess tomorrow. Speaking of tomorrow, we have to figure out sleeping arrangements for tonight." Viv looked directly at Christy and Trevor.

"I can bunk in with you in your folks' room," Christy said quickly. "Eric and Trevor can fight over who gets the couch and who gets the guest room." She looked to Trevor. "The couch by the fire is bigger, but the other one folds out to a queen."

"Thanks," he said, trying not to smile over her quick summation of who would sleep where, in case anyone got the wrong idea.

No one said anything else and when Christy looked back at Viv and Eric, they were both smiling at her. And Trevor. "What?" she demanded.

"Oh, nothing," Viv said with a knowing grin, then pushed back and stood, gathering her dishes. "Another glass of wine anyone?"

Eric shook his head, but stood as well and stacked plates. "Let me help."

Christy started to gather things, but Eric shooed her away. "I've got it. Why don't you and Trevor check on the fire?"

Meaning "Why don't you and Trevor get lost," Trevor thought, but he couldn't blame the guy. Viv was a captive audience for the night and he'd want to spend as much time alone with her as he could. Viv seemed to be dealing with it and wasn't signaling for a rescue, so he smiled and said, "You guys cooked. Let me and Christy clean up. I think the fire needs a few more logs."

Christy shot him a look, but when she glanced to Viv, her friend didn't say anything, so she forced a smile and said, "I'm not good at cooking, but I can sterilize with the best of 'em."

"Thanks, guys," Viv said, then followed Eric into the living-room area.

Christy watched them leave, frowning.

"They're just building a fire," Trevor assured her.

"Yeah, that's what worries me." She looked at him. "And you're right there, fanning the flames."

"Viv's a grown woman. And I didn't see her crying for help there. In fact, she seemed sincerely grateful to have some more alone time with Eric."

Christy didn't say anything; she just turned her attention back to cleaning the table.

He followed her into the kitchen with a stack of dishes. "Christy—"

She deposited her pile on the counter and turned on him. "I know she's a grown woman. But I also know how charming Eric can be when he wants to be. You weren't there when he walked away from her. I was. You didn't sit up nights with her on the phone. You didn't spend hours over coffee breaks at work listening to her pour her soul out. You didn't watch her try to function without falling apart every other minute. For months. Months, Trevor. So don't tell me how wonderful it would be if they got back together." She blew out another breath and turned away.

Gently he turned her back, working not to smile when she shrugged away from his touch.

"And don't smile at me," she warned him, apparently seeing him as clearly as he saw her.

"No, ma'am."

"This isn't funny. And it's not some game. It's—"

"I know. Which is why I wouldn't dare risk life or limb telling you how cute you look when you're mad." He held up his hands when she snatched up the salad tongs and snapped them in his direction. "See? So I didn't say that." He put his hand on hers and lowered the tongs. "What I do see is how loyal a friend you are and I think Viv couldn't be luckier than to have such a staunch supporter on her side." He took the tongs from her. "But ultimately, you also know it's her decision."

Christy grumbled, but didn't say anything. Finally she turned away and flipped on the water in the sink. "Well, it doesn't mean I have to like it," she muttered.

He stood behind her, enjoying the hell out of her, moods and all, wanting to touch her, but unsure if she'd appreciate his touch at the moment.

"I just don't want her hurt," Christy said softly as she scrubbed away at the plates.

Trevor grabbed a towel when she thrust the first dripping-wet plate at him. "I understand that."

"She deserves to be happy." Another plate got shoved his way.

He took that one and wiped it down quickly. "We all deserve happiness." He stacked the plate on the first one just in time to snag the next. "Even Eric, right?"

She jerked her gaze to his, opening her mouth to blast him for sure, but her motion sent a few soap suds flying, one of which landed on the end of her nose. "Well, I can hardly be taken seriously now, can I?" she said instead, still glaring at him.

And he simply had no choice. None at all. He dropped the dish towel on the counter and leaned down and kissed her. She didn't respond. In fact, she froze in place, as if she hadn't seen it coming. And he couldn't blame her. He hadn't, either, until she made him do it.

He lifted his head and she just blinked at him. "You have foam on your nose now, too," she said after a moment.

"Yes, ma'am," he said, knowing he was smiling and not caring.

"Why did you do that?" she asked, still standing stock-still, one hand plunged in the sudsy water.

"Because I had to know."

"What? What did you have to know?"

"How that incredible, smart mouth of yours tasted."

That seemed to set her back for a moment. Good, he thought. Maybe more people needed to set her back, make her think. But only he needed to be the one doing it by kissing her.

"And?" she asked, after another long moment.

He laughed. "And I think I need another reconnaissance mission, gather more data, before I can file my report."

"Ah." She turned back to the dishes, as if nothing had happened.

Now he was the one set back for a moment. How did she manage to do that? "What ah?" he demanded. "Ah, okay? Or ah, no thanks?"

She smiled and handed him another plate. "Just ah."

Great. "Christy—"

"Shut up and dry the dishes, Trevor."

He snatched the last plate from her and tried to decide how he was going to handle this...this whatever it was he was having with her. Because he wanted to kiss her again, taste her again, and dammit he wanted her to kiss him back. Was he really so out of touch with the normal day-to-day stuff that he'd forgotten how to seduce a woman?

He almost laughed at that. If he could have planned the worst possible way to seduce a woman, today couldn't have been any more on target. First he'd kidnapped her, in her underwear no less, forced her to parade around in a god-awful dress, left her to sleep on a porch swing, then accompanied her to a cabin where two people who'd hurt each other enough to get divorced were forced to spend the night under the same roof. The same two people she wanted to keep apart. Sort of hard to mount a seduction campaign when his target was actively working to douse the flames of the other couple. Not the most romantic of atmospheres.

She helped him dry and put the dishes away, then they both stood there uncertainly. "I'm not sure if we should intrude." Christy craned her neck around the bar. "They're sitting on the couch in front of the fire. Talking." She leaned back against the counter and folded her arms.

"Is that so bad?" Trevor asked quietly. "I mean, if nothing else, maybe they'll get a few things straightened out, mend some fences."

Christy snorted. "It's going to take some mighty strong lumber for that."

Trevor hitched himself up on the counter. "What happened? Between them, I mean. You said something about him putting his career first."

Christy nodded. "Viv had just been promoted, about three months after the wedding. Eric is an international investment banker. They bought a house, big enough for the family they planned to start a couple of years down the line. Everything was great. They really seemed to complement each other. Everyone thought things were perfect, including me."

"How did it fall apart so quickly then?"

"Well, Eric was always a bit domineering, but Viv was a good match for him, or so I thought. She has a great sense of humor and could usually tease him around to her way of thinking. Of course, in hindsight, we all realize he got his way more often enough than not." She sighed. "Then about six months into the marriage he gets an offer to relocate to Sweden."

"Sweden?"

"Yeah, his parents are here but his grandparents are there and his granddad is involved in some kind of venture-capital thing. Anyway, they wanted Eric and Viv to move there, have their family there."

"In Sweden."

She nodded.

"It's not that unusual," Trevor said. "I mean, military families relocate all over the world. Kids turn out okay."

"I don't see you dragging a wife and little ones around with you," Christy said pointedly.

"Point taken," he admitted. "It's certainly not for everyone, but if his opportunity was a good one—"

"She didn't marry into the military," Christy said, "so she had no way to see this coming. She just started her career here. Her family is here. She'd just bought a house, just gotten married for Pete's sake."

"Couldn't she work as a nurse in Sweden?"

"That wasn't the point, but no. She doesn't speak Swedish and it would mean not only learning the language, but schooling all over again over there and starting from the bottom. The medical community is run entirely differently and—"

"And he was asking her to give up everything for him."

Christy stopped and blew out a breath. "Exactly."

"She wasn't even willing to give it a try?"

"She'd have had to leave her job here, with no guarantee. Sell the house she was halfway done decorating. Leave her family and her friends. And let's remember, this wasn't exactly Eric's dream job. Nor was it so he could go back to the homeland to be with his family and friends. He'd visited his grandparents a handful of times as a child and that was it. It was a risky venture and he was walking away from a far more certain financial future here because the idea excited him. He literally asked her to jump off a cliff with him and hope for the best."

"And she said no."

"After a lot of tears and soul-searching, she said no. She asked him to stay here, to live the life they'd planned on, be happy the way they had been."

"And he said no."

She nodded. "He was angry that she wouldn't see that his career and choices were most important. He honestly felt that it was the wife's duty to support her husband's choices, that he was the supporter financially and she emotionally."

Trevor smiled. "Oh, I imagine that went over well."

"That's just it. Viv is a pretty traditional type. She felt a tremendous amount of guilt for standing up for what she wanted, for saying it was equally important to his wants and needs. It hurt her terribly when he basically decided this new venture was more important than her and their marriage."

"Do you really think that's what he thought?"

"No. He thought she'd cave and run after him. And when she didn't he got angry and said some things that were really unforgivable. And, admittedly, so did she. After that, neither of them would back down, not without denting their pride."

Trevor looked to the living area. "Do you think he's really changed? Enough that they could work things out?"

Christy shrugged. "My instinct is to say no. I mean, it's been a year and a half, and I will admit that he has tried several times to talk to her. But this crushed Viv and she simply couldn't allow him back into her life, not even a little bit. She sold the house, along with most everything in it, bought the little place she has now and started over. She never wanted to see or talk to him again and I don't blame her."

"So Kate stepped in."

Christy rolled her eyes. "Miss Helpful."

"Her heart was in the right place. At least, she had no harmful intentions."

"I know, but she shouldn't have done it."

"They *are* talking. Maybe in the long run, it wasn't such a bad thing."

Christy scowled, then nodded. "And I hate admitting that, so don't rub it in."

Trevor grinned. "You suffered the most, so you have every right to be mad."

Christy sank down to the floor, leaning back against the cabinets. "I'm not mad, not really. Just concerned."

Trevor hopped down and slid to sit across from her, stretching out his legs alongside hers. "And tired. I still feel terrible about my part in all this."

She cocked her head. "Just how did Kate manage to talk you into it anyway? You don't strike me as the type to be bullied into anything."

"I would have agreed with you. But you've never been trapped in a tiny room with a crying bride, half an hour before she's supposed to marry your best friend. Ten minutes and I was ready to do whatever it took to make her stop crying."

Christy laughed. "I suppose I can see your terror."

Trevor tipped his foot to one side and nudged her calf. "I meant what I said. About making it up to you."

He felt her leg tense, but she relaxed and didn't move away. In fact, she smiled at him in that dry way of hers. "What exactly is the standard compensation for kidnapping?"

He laughed. "I think that's usually up to the abductee. How about I offer to be your personal thunderstorm hotline for the next...well, however long you think the detail should last?"

Her gaze caught his then and he felt his heart slow until he could feel each individual thump.

"That's—" Her voice was rough and she paused to clear her throat.

Trevor swallowed, glad to know that he wasn't the only one affected by their close proximity to one another.

"A good start," she finished.

"I can think of another thing I could do to show you how sorry I am."

Her throat worked and she folded her arms beneath her breasts, the action bringing her nipples to his attention as they pressed against the front of her sweatshirt. And it wasn't remotely cold where they were sitting. Which meant she was reacting to him.

"What would that be?" she asked a bit hoarsely.

Now or never, he told himself. He scooted forward until he was right next to her. "That would be this." He cupped her face with one hand and leaned in and kissed her. Only this time he didn't plan on being the only one doing the kissing.

8

His lips were warm, and soft and firm at the same time. He tasted like wine. It was a heady mix and it clouded her brain. But it felt too damn good, so she let it.

She hadn't seen it coming last time...but he'd made it perfectly clear this time. And she still wasn't prepared for it. Or for him.

"Let me in," he murmured against her lips. "I want to taste you."

She shuddered with pleasure, right there on the kitchen floor. And she parted her lips and let him in. He kept the kiss slow, and easy...almost lazy. Like he had all night.

And she supposed they did. Dear God, could she imagine kissing him like this, all slow and lazy and hot, for hours? Why, yes, she realized, she absolutely could. In fact, her body was way past imagining and begging her to make it happen.

She leaned into his kiss when he teased her tongue into his own mouth. Wrapping her hand around the back of his neck, she sighed when his long fingers slid into her hair. Her entire body felt electrified at his touch, all tingly and hypersensitive.

Her fingertips traced the edge of his collar as his mouth left hers and trailed hot, wet kisses along her jaw. She dipped her fingers below his collar, brushing his warm skin, wondering what it would feel like to run her hands down his broad back. His naked broad back.

Someone moaned. She was pretty sure it was her. She pulled back, sliding her hand from his neck and curling her fingers into her palm, and against the need to touch him. "Trevor."

He lifted his lips from where they'd been making devastating headway toward the tender skin of her neck. But he stayed a breath away. "What?"

"We're sitting on the kitchen floor." And another second or two, she might not have been sitting any longer.

"And?"

"And we probably shouldn't be."

He lifted his head and looked at her, amusement and desire both in his eyes. It was like a one-two punch directly to her libido.

"Where should we be?" he asked, clearly in no hurry to stop what he'd been doing.

"I—" She laughed. "I refuse to answer on the grounds that it might incriminate me." *And get me naked.* Which, if there weren't two people in the other room, she might have very easily allowed. And it was that realization that had her scooting away from him. Him and his blue eyes and lazy, warm lips and amused smile.

He let her slide away, but there was a promise in

his eyes. *I always succeed. Eventually.* It made her shiver in anticipation.

"I think I like that answer," he said. "A lot. As intriguing as the woman who uttered it."

Intriguing? He thought she was intriguing? "I think I'm flattered." *And incredibly hot for you.* But she didn't think it was wise to add that part. Since he could probably read the neon sign over her head saying the same thing. She wanted to fan herself as he continued to stare at her.

Well, you said you wanted him, she thought. *And he's all right here, ready to be had.* Yeah, well, she hadn't thought things out that far. She wasn't sure what she'd do with him once she had him. Well, that was a lie. She knew exactly what she wanted to do with him. But now was not the time or the place. And she'd just met him, for God's sake!

So why was it that the time frame made absolutely no difference in this instance? Why was it she felt they'd been more deeply involved since the moment he woke her up, than some of the men she'd dated for months? A day with him felt like a year with anyone else. Not that she'd ever spent a year with anyone else, but still.

He rolled to a graceful stand, surprising for how big a man he was, then reached a hand to help her up and pull her thankfully from those disturbing thoughts.

She looked at the long-fingered hand he'd offered her and flashed again on all the things she wanted him to do to her with those fingers. She wasn't sure if she wanted to risk taking hold of them at that moment. She might do something really embarrassing, like yank him down on top of her and her rioting hormones. Maybe that was all this was. She just needed to have a hormone tune-up. After all, she'd been working hard. And there hadn't been too many starving artists or boring office managers in her life of late. Just a brief little tune-up, that was all she needed.

But she was too busy for…for whatever it was she saw him offering in those blue eyes of his.

Steeling herself and her raging hormones, she took his hand, and it felt like a hot brand against her palm. She let go as soon as she was upright, certain the room was spinning only because she'd stood up too fast. Surely that was it.

"Steady there," he said, putting his hands on her shoulders.

She wanted to grab them and yank them down a bit, to where she ached to have him touch her. Only, first she'd need to get rid of all her clothes. And his.

She turned to the sink and flipped on the water. *Cool off, Christy.* The man will think you're a sex maniac. She snorted under her breath. *Yeah, that will drive him away.*

Which brought her to the real problem at hand. Sure, okay, she wanted his body. In the worst way. And the best. And she was pretty damn sure she could have it, maybe even repeatedly. But the real truth was she didn't want just a brief tune-up. Not with him.

So what if she was busy? He intrigued her, too. More than anyone she'd ever met. And if they started with the sex part, maybe she'd never get to the what-might-come-next part. In fact, she had no idea how to get to that part. But she was pretty sure she should find out before she did anything else with him. No matter how good it might feel. Dammit.

"You two going to stay in there all night?" Vivian called out. "The fire feels good."

So do Trevor's hands, Christy thought. She had to clear her throat, twice. "Yeah, just a minute." Trevor reached around her and turned off the water she'd never gotten around to splashing on her cheeks. Not that it would have helped. She wanted desperately to lean back into him, feel him all big and strong behind her.

He turned her slowly around, keeping her pinned between that big, delicious body of his and the counter behind her. "I think I can file that report now."

"Report? Oh. *That* report." She trembled, wishing his little reconnaissance mission hadn't ended so abruptly. *Jesus, make up your mind.* Only, she couldn't think straight. He looked at her like...like no one had ever looked at her. He tied up her tongue and made her heart pound. She wanted to taste him again. And not just his mouth.

"Ahh," he said, drawing out the word. "That's what it was."

"Ah what?"

He grinned down at her. "Just ahhhhhh."

"Oh." Dear God, she might come if he made that sound one more time.

He leaned in. "Exactly."

She struggled to remember why it was that going straight to the sex part wasn't a good idea. The hell with Vivian and Eric.

Somehow, a shred of control asserted itself. "We'd better get into the living room. They'll be wondering."

"They can wonder for another moment, then." And he dipped his head and kissed her again, kissed her as though he simply had the right to do it. Whenever and wherever he pleased.

She should be setting him straight. Pushing him away. Telling him all the reasons why it was important that they know each other better first. But that didn't explain why she felt as though she'd known him forever. And why his mouth felt so right on hers. Why his possession of her was as natural as breathing. They needed to talk about all that, she decided, figure it all out. And they would. In just another moment.

"Well, don't let me interrupt anything."

Christy jumped and jerked her mouth from his, but Trevor just lifted his head slowly and smiled at Vivian. "Not a problem."

"No, I can see that," she said, grinning at them both.

"Vivian—" Christy began, feeling horribly guilty without quite knowing why.

"I just wanted to tell you that I'm heading to bed," she said.

"But the fire—"

"Is still there. I thought you two might enjoy it. Eric is going to take the guest room. Is that okay, Trevor?"

"I can sleep anywhere. Thank you for putting me up for the night."

She smiled. "Not a problem."

Christy slipped out from between the counter and Trevor. "I'll come on with you." Surely Viv would want to talk and that was the reason Christy had come up here, right? To support her friend. Not to make out in the kitchen. Though damn if her body agreed with that assessment.

"That's okay. Christy, I—"

But she knew Vivian too well. Sure, she wouldn't have minded if her friend stayed by the fire. She knew Viv would want her to have fun. She was her best friend, after all. But Christy saw the weariness in her eyes that had nothing to do with physical fatigue. "I want to."

"I can tend the fire," Trevor offered.

"Okay, then. If you're sure." Vivian thanked him and headed to the master bedroom.

Christy looked back to him, a hundred thoughts in her head, but not one of them would form on her lips. "Good night." It seemed such a lame thing to say when there was so much more to be said between them. But whatever that was would have to wait until later. Vivian came first.

"'Night, Christy." His smile told her he understood, which only made her body riot harder.

The walk to the bedroom was the longest of her life, and she could feel him watching her. Her body felt it like a caress...a long, slow one. Her knees were trembling by the time she got to the bedroom door.

Vivian pounced the moment she closed it behind her, shutting Trevor out, but not the effect he had on her.

"Oh. My. God," Viv swore, fanning her face. "I swear the air shimmered around you two, things were so hot." She sat cross-legged on the bed, suddenly not sounding so tired. "Tell me every last single detail."

Christy laughed in disbelief. "I didn't come in here to talk about Trevor." Thank God, since she'd probably sound like a babbling idiot if she tried. "I figured you'd want to talk about...everything."

Vivian made a face. "I'm tired of talking." She wiggled her eyebrows. "Besides, your story looks to be much more entertaining than mine." She patted the bed. "Sit and tell."

Christy sank onto the bed. "I don't know what there is to tell, really. I just met him."

Viv laughed. "Yeah, I could tell you were still in that awkward get-to-know-you stage when I walked into the kitchen."

Christy laughed, too, then shrugged, half-embarrassed, which was silly since she and Viv shared everything. "I can't explain it. He's like...well he's not like anyone I've ever met."

Viv scooted closer. "Sounds promising."

"I don't know what it is."

"But you know what it isn't."

"What do you mean?"

"We've been friends for what, four years now? Five? And close friends for almost all of that. It's not like you to just jump into anything intimate. In fact, I'd say quite the opposite."

What could she say to that? Viv was right. "So? I've dated, I've had my share of fun. Now I have a job that's demanding, a life I enjoy, friends. It just doesn't make any sense to let someone have that kind of access to me until I'm sure it's...something more than a few dates."

"Exactly what I meant. Trevor's not a few dates. Which you already know or I wouldn't have seen what I saw in my own kitchen."

Christy started to argue, then shrugged helplessly. "There is something. I can't explain. Like I said, he's different. When we talk, or joke, or...I don't know, even jab at each other...it's like we've been trading those little amusing jabs for years. Lifetimes."

Viv nodded. "Remember you asked me once if I believed in soul mates?"

"Oh, no. Trevor might be intriguing and he definitely got my attention in a way that no man ever has, but then kidnapping tends to have that effect. Besides, if I recall, at that time we were discussing the man who is currently sleeping in your guest room."

Vivian frowned and Christy felt a moment's guilt for bringing Eric into this, but they were going to talk about him eventually.

"We were. And I thought Eric was my soul mate."

"*Was* being the operative word."

Vivian didn't respond to that. Instead, she said, "You told me you didn't believe there was one person who could just click into you so deeply that you knew the moment you met him he was the one." She studied her friend. "Can you look me in the eye and tell me you still feel that way?"

Christy thought about that moment in the chapel when Trevor had looked into her eyes and told her he wished they had met under different circumstances. There had been something there. Something there again when he'd kissed her, touched her, looked at her. She honestly didn't know how to answer the question, so she turned it back on her friend. "Do you?"

"If you'd asked me eighteen months ago, when Eric left for Sweden, I'd have sworn I was wrong. Because a soul mate wouldn't hurt his own soul mate so badly. And if you'd asked me yesterday, I'd have probably said the same thing."

Christy's eyes widened. "But today?"

"But today maybe the reason it still hurts so badly, eighteen months and a whole lot of growth and understanding later, is because the connection was so strong, so important, so right to begin with. So the destruction of that connection would have to hurt that bad...maybe forever." She looked at Christy and her eyes started to water. "Because we are soul mates. So it's the one connection that truly mattered. And I let it go."

Viv started to cry and Christy scooted across the bed and folded her into her arms. "Oh, sweetie, I'm so sorry." She stroked her hair. "I'm sorry I let him get to you. I knew I should have wrung Kate's chiffon-covered—"

Viv struggled to sit up and wiped at her face. "No, no, that's not what I'm saying. I'm saying that I had to do this, talk to him, see him again. I've been miserable without him, Christy."

"You were miserable with him," Christy reminded her friend, alarmed at where this was going. One day in each other's presence and Viv was a wreck again. This couldn't be good.

"Only when he left. Not when we were together."

"But he did leave, Viv. I'm not trying to be cruel, but you're talking about soul mates and how they are meant to be together above all else...but he chose a career move over you, his wife. His supposed soul mate. I'm not so sure I think there's any such thing. Just human beings fumbling their way through life and sometimes hurting the people who love them best, maybe even the ones they love, as well. But he screwed up, Viv. Are you honestly saying you think he deserves another chance? How can you be sure when push comes to shove, he won't choose something for himself over you again?"

She sniffed and rubbed her nose. "I'm saying that I expected to feel hurt and pain and anger if I ever saw him again, and I felt all three of those in spades. And spewed them all over him, to be sure."

"You already put yourself through all that. Is it really right for him to force you through it again?"

"That's just it. I went through it all with my therapist, with you, with my parents, but never with the one person that I needed to go through it all with."

Christy couldn't deny that. Eric had left, Viv had filed for divorce and he hadn't contested it. It had all been handled distantly, cold and detached and emotionless. At least between the two main parties. Viv hadn't been at all emotionless about it. She had no idea how Eric had handled it.

At the time Christy thought it was best that way, a swift death would leave her friend more whole, more capable of grieving and healing than a long, protracted ugly affair. And while she still felt that way, in general, she couldn't deny that maybe it would have been cathartic to get all those emotions out and directed to the only person they mattered to. Christy said as much to Viv.

Viv raked her hair from her face and blew out a long breath. "I don't think so," she said, surprisingly. "Not then, anyway. I don't think there was any good way for it to end at that time. We were so confused and full of pride and hurt. Lord knows I suffered and made those who love me suffer, as well."

Christy grabbed her hand. "We love you. We'd do it again."

She sniffled. "I know, I know." She gave a watery laugh. "And you might have to, after this."

Christy frowned. "What are you saying?"

Viv took a deep breath and smiled, though it was a bit wobbly. "We miss each other, Christy. I'm mad at him for the choice he made and the hurt he caused me. But I wasn't completely blameless. And also...I still love him."

"Why?" Christy swore under her breath. "Don't answer that. I'm just...angry. Angry that he can just waltz back in here almost two years later and you're willing to forgive and forget."

Now Viv turned sharp. "I didn't say that. I can't forget. But as to forgiveness...well, maybe it's not forgiveness as much as willingness to try."

"Try to do what?"

"Spend time together." She smiled again, and this time it reached her eyes. "Find out if we're more miserable together than we were apart."

Christy smiled then, too, or tried to. "Is it worth it? Risking all the pain and heartache again?"

"I'm already in pain. My heart already aches. I've learned how to function, to live, to move on. But we loved each other for a reason. For a hundred reasons, a thousand. And maybe we were both just too stubborn to fight for those reasons. Or maybe we just made stupid mistakes."

"We?"

She nodded. "I know Eric made the decision to go to Sweden. But I'm the one who filed for divorce because of it. We never discussed it. I threatened, he walked, we split."

"But—"

"And I refused to discuss it with him after. Even though he begged me to later on."

"After it was too late," Christy snorted.

"I'm not so sure there is such a thing. What I do know is that we were both stubborn. Him for thinking I should just pack up and follow my man, and me for refusing to discuss it after he left, when he realized he was miserable alone."

"He should be miserable."

Vivian smiled sadly. "So we should both be punished forever for being too stupid and stubborn to try and find another way?"

Christy sighed. "Of course not. I just—"

"You just don't want to see me hurt. I know, and I love you for it. But well, this time I think my eyes are more open. And my heart a bit more humble."

"He tread on it pretty heavily."

"And instead of trying to mend it, I tread as heavily as I could on his. Two wrongs and all that..."

Christy didn't say anything—she was still trying to come to terms with everything Viv had told her. Finally she rolled her eyes and let out a weak laugh.

Viv reached out and lightly punched her arm. "What's so funny?"

"Well, after all this I'm thinking it might be wise to just cut my losses where Trevor is concerned and run like hell. This love stuff is way too complicated, with too much opportunity for pain and grief."

"Yeah, but along with the potential for pain and grief is the kind of love and soul-deep satisfaction you can only have if you take the risk."

"And after all this you still think it's worth the risk?"

Viv smiled, a knowing smile that actually stirred a wisp of envy in Christy. "Yeah," she said softly. "I think I do."

9

CHRISTY PUSHED through the doors of Richmond General Monday afternoon, unable to escape the feeling that her entire world had somehow been tilted on its side. How could things feel so monumentally different in only seventy-two hours?

Eric and Trevor had left the cabin early yesterday morning after breakfast, while she had stayed on with Viv. She'd also purposely avoided being alone with Trevor, confused by all the things Viv had said, about the way she felt when she looked at him.

About the way he made her feel when he looked at her.

She'd gone home to Viv's last night, then stopped by her place to change before work today. The workmen would be finishing up her floors by the end of today, so she could reclaim her own bed when she got off shift tomorrow morning.

Viv was already on shift and they'd planned to have dinner in the cafeteria together if Christy could swing it, but Viv had left a message canceling earlier. She was going out with Eric when she got off work tonight. Just dinner and conversation, she'd stipulated, but Christy still worried about her. Viv wasn't in ICU tonight, she'd been floated to Emergency, so now she probably wouldn't see her until sometime tomorrow.

Christy rode the elevator to the second-floor ICU unit, wondering if she and Trevor could keep a dinner date to just food and simple conversation. Her entire body had ached as she'd watched him drive away yesterday morning. Why had she kept herself away from him all morning? Just one touch, one kiss. But no, she'd told herself distance was best until she figured out what she was feeling. Well, she had a whole bunch of distance now and what had that done for her and her aching hormones? Zip. She should have jumped the guy when she had the chance.

That kiss... It had followed her into her dreams, dreams that hadn't included Vivian's interruption. She sighed and forced him out of her thoughts—again—as the doors slid open. She had a twelve-hour shift ahead of her and doubted it would run smoothly. They never did. She'd need all her thoughts focused on the job at hand, and not on visions of what Trevor's hands could have been doing if she'd stayed with him by that fire. Instead of talking to Viv about soul mates...and giving love a chance. Love. She snorted. What she had was a serious case of lust. *But what could it be if you gave it a chance?* her little voice persisted as she waved and greeted Jolie and Sam, her shift mates for the night.

Since she hadn't given Trevor her phone number, and more important, he hadn't asked for it, or asked about where she lived…it was probably all a moot point. The storm, the cozy cabin, the odd circumstances of their acquaintance…that's all it had been. He was off starting a whole new life for himself. He had no more time for her than she did for him. But instead of feeling relieved, she felt sort of depressed.

Pasting a smile on her face, she forced a teasing note into her voice as she faced her co-workers. "So, ladies and germs, what fun and frivolity are on tap for us tonight?"

"That's what we want to know, girlfriend," Jolie responded, her full lips curved in a wide, knowing smile as she gave Christy a head to toe once-over.

"What?" Christy asked, looking down at herself. She looked normal enough. Surely her preoccupation with a certain former lieutenant commander wasn't written all over her face.

"Just that someone must have had some fun and frivolity over the weekend," Sam said, folding his arms and leaning his long, lanky frame against the nurses' station counter.

"What—what makes you say that?" Christy felt her cheeks heat up. Dammit. She hadn't done anything. And even if she had, what could they possibly know about it? Unless— "What did Viv tell you guys?"

Sam smirked at Jolie and held out his hand. "Five bucks."

Jolie huffed, ignoring his outstretched hand. "Tell me you didn't," she said to Christy. "I had faith in you. Which is more than I can say for Easy Fly Boy here."

Sam just laughed. "Yeah, five dollars worth of faith. Hand it over, *girlfriend*," he said, in a dead-on impersonation of her.

Christy looked at them both and shook her head. "I have no idea what you two are talking about. I spent the weekend with Viv at her folks' cabin—"

"With some guy named Trevor?" Jolie supplied.

Christy's mouth dropped open, then snapped shut. "How did you—? Oh, I'm going to kill Viv."

"We haven't seen Viv. She's downstairs. But there is a little matter of a bouquet that was delivered about thirty minutes ago."

"Bouquet? Delivered?" Christy pushed her hair off her forehead. "What are you talking about?" But her heart was pounding.

Sam ducked behind the counter and pulled out an obscene spray of gorgeous flowers spilling out of a tall crystal vase. He clasped a hand over his chest as he set them on the counter and, with great drama, read the card. "'The thunder wasn't all outside the cabin. Trevor.'" He sighed deeply. "All the good ones are straight. I swear."

"Give me that." Christy snatched the card from his hand and read it. She had no idea what Trevor's handwriting looked like, but this didn't look like florist handwriting. He'd not only taken the time to send her flowers, but apparently he'd gone personally and picked them out. She shouldn't be impressed, shouldn't be bowled over. She definitely shouldn't be smiling and wanting to do a little conga dance all around the ICU. After all, hadn't she just decided it was better if they left it at an interesting weekend and got on with their lives? Their separate lives?

But she wanted to do that conga dance. She managed to tamp down the urge, but only because Jolie and Sam were both standing there, waiting. She managed an aloof shrug instead. "He's a friend of Viv's friend Kate. There was a little mix-up this weekend at her wedding. It was nice of him to send flowers."

Jolie snorted. "It was more than nice. What's up with the thunder and the cabin? And don't deny it, missy, because when Sam read his name off that card...well, the look on your face alone cost me five bucks. He must have been something if Miss I-Don't-Sleep-Around went up to a cabin with him."

"You actually call me that?" Christy asked, then smacked Jolie lightly on the arm when she nodded in complete seriousness. "Since when is my love life a topic of conversation around here?"

"Never," Sam said solemnly, then grinned. "Your lack of one, now *that* we talk about."

"Exactly! So why the stupid nickname when men aren't exactly lining up trying to get me to throw away the title?"

"Half of them you don't notice and the other half...well..." Sam rolled his eyes. "Not all the bad ones are gay, if you know what I'm saying."

"Hey, now, don't go criticizing my choice in dates."

"Yeah, it's not like she has a lot of time to sift through the pile of applicants," Jolie added. "Or the pile she might have if she didn't work a million hours a week."

Christy snorted. "Trust me, the lack of applicants, as you call them, has nothing to do with my work schedule. And as for who I do pick—" she eyed Sam "—you have little room to talk."

Jolie laughed and Sam didn't even try to defend himself. "Hey, I kid because I love," he said, giving her his best puppy-dog look.

Christy rolled her eyes, then went over to the flowers. They were truly stunning. "And for your information," she added, taking a deep sniff, "I didn't sleep with him." She grinned at Sam. "So *you* can pay up, buster. Teach you to keep your nose, and your bets, out of my love life."

He just laughed. "Why on earth would we do that, darling? Now that you've finally gotten one?"

Christy's gaze narrowed. "They're flowers. That's all. I just met the guy."

"Yeah, well, I wish the guys I just met would send me flowers that looked like those," Sam said, all dreamy.

Jolie rolled her eyes. "Well, if you'd date the ones old enough to have jobs, maybe—"

Sam plinked her on the arm with a pen, then rushed off when a buzzer at the desk went off. "I'll get you back for that one, sister."

Jolie just laughed. "Yeah, yeah. I'm scared." Then she turned her knowing look at Christy. "So, don't spare any of the juicy stuff." She wiggled her fingers beckoningly. "Us married girls still need our cheap thrills, you know what I'm sayin'?"

"Yeah, I hear what you're saying, all right," Christy said dryly. "And you wouldn't believe me if I told you." She pushed past her to get to the charts.

"Oh, now you've got to tell me. I get dibs as your dinner date this evening."

Christy grinned. "Yeah, and you're buying, with Sam's five bucks."

"Sold," she said, rushing off as another beeper sounded.

Christy shook her head and started going through the charts to see what they had on the unit tonight. But her gaze kept straying to the flowers. *The thunder wasn't all outside the cabin.* An undeniably delicious shiver of pleasure washed over her, and since she was alone, she danced a brief two-step, smiled to herself, then got to work.

TREVOR LOOKED at the wiring he'd had put in for the separate classrooms. "I have to have recessed lighting and enough power to run video and—"

"It's all there, boss," Jimmy said. He was a good twenty-five years or more older than Trevor, gruff, plain spoken, former military himself. An all-around handyman that Trevor had noticed advertised in the local paper. He'd talked to the old drill sergeant for five minutes and knew he'd found the

right guy. Convincing Jimmy of that had taken another fifteen minutes. Jimmy was more actively re-
tired than actively seeking work. The ad had been
his wife's idea, he'd told Trevor, a way to get him
out of her house. Her house, he'd repeated disgust-
edly. Like he hadn't paid for the damn thing and all
the other little trinkets she liked to collect, he'd com-
plained.

The tirade had gone on for another ten minutes
while Trevor listened politely, grinning to himself
the whole time. Jimmy liked to grunt and groan, but
it was obvious to anyone who really listened how
much he loved the woman he bought all those trinkets for. He was also intrigued by Trevor's business
venture, and had eventually grudgingly agreed
when Trevor asked him to help out.

"I laid enough wire in the army to light up a
damn continent," Jimmy grumbled. "You can run
whatever you like through here. No problem." He
stood and scratched at his thinning hair. "You still
planning on starting your first class in two weeks?"

"Is that a problem?" Trevor asked, knowing he'd
get a snarl from the old guy.

"Not on my end, pup. You get your tables and
chairs and pads and what have you in here. I'll get
your power on."

"Inspector is coming Thursday."

"I'll be ready for the damned busybody. All a
bunch of—" He chomped down on the unlit stub of
a cigar he always had clamped in his teeth, leaving
Trevor to fill in the rest of the sentence.

He was still grinning as Jimmy went back to work. For all the guy hadn't wanted the job, he worked harder than three men half his age would have with very few demands. So Trevor put up with a little griping. He liked people with character, and Jimmy had truckloads of it. "I've got a truck coming in fifteen minutes," he said, "so I'm heading down to the loading dock. Call me if you need me."

"I can take care of myself. Don't need you looking over my shoulder every other minute."

"Yes, sir, sergeant, sir." He chuckled as he headed down the stairs, Jimmy's response still coloring the air blue.

McQuillen Enterprises consisted of two large metal warehouses and about ten acres of partially wooded property, all surrounded by a twelve-foot-high chain-link fence. The whole operation was out in the middle of nowhere, the only part of a failed industrial center that had never been fully developed. About a fifteen-minute drive from Richmond proper, ten minutes off the highway and a half hour from the airport, it was accessible, yet tucked away. Perfect for his needs.

Trevor had sectioned off one of the warehouses, insulated it, put in walls and ceilings, plumbing and carpeting, turning it into a handful of executive classrooms and offices. His plan was to operate solo, at least for the time being. He had put the word out to a few other former special-ops pals and was fairly confident it wouldn't be too long before a few would come on board and help him out when the business began to expand. And he had a feeling that demand would happen sooner rather than later if the initial response to his classes was any indication. He already received several contract proposals to look over, and if they went well, he knew he'd be busy quickly.

He crossed the lot to the other warehouse. This one he'd kept more basic, filled with padded floors, some padded walls, all sorts of lighting that could duplicate any number of natural or physical situations that his men might find themselves in. Bright daylight, dusk, moonlight, fog, even headlights bearing down on them. He had plans for an outside course and a firing range, but those would have to wait for now.

He rolled up the bay door and looked inside the dimly lit building. The floor padding was in and most of the lighting done. Some of the teaching equipment was in, but there was more on order. Padded suits, workout dummies, hard plastic knives, batons. The list went on and on. But when you were sending men into areas of the world whose only background in setting up police forces was based on military and rebel regimes, you had to prepare them to face any and every possibility. He knew firsthand that most of those possibilities would be probabilities.

He would also be training the men who would be protecting those who went to teach, as well as others, such as executives trying to bring commerce to these countries and not trained personally in defense.

The sad part was that there was such a demand for this type of training facility. And probably always would be. He'd begun work on this several years before, when the realization for the need to do this as a private, rather than military, enterprise had become obvious. Even the military realized this and were some of the first in line to send business his way. So he'd calculated the need, made contacts, gotten funding, used his own savings...and taken the leap.

He watched the truck rumble up containing chairs, desks and some of the training equipment he'd ordered. He'd done his duty to his country and was proud of his service in the armed forces. But he was energized in a way he'd never been before at the prospect of continuing that dedication, but as his own boss.

"Right here," he directed the truck, waving his arms. Yes, his own boss. His own life. His own man. He was ready. More than ready.

Christy's face popped into his mind, as it managed to do now at the oddest times. He wondered if she'd gotten the flowers. He hoped she liked them. Hoped she liked his note.

"Sir?"

Trevor snapped out of his reverie to find the truck driver leaning out his window, clipboard in hand.

"Sorry," he said, taking the clipboard and signing

his name in a scrawl by the X. "A million things on my mind."

The truck driver just shrugged and took the clipboard back.

Trevor shook his head, smiling at himself as he walked to the back of the truck to help unload it. *Better get your mind out of Christy Russell's life and into your own.*

He had two weeks to do about two months' worth of work. But he had sixteen men coming for his first class and he'd be damned if he'd postpone it. They were all slated to head to Kosovo four months from now, and after a week here they'd be a whole helluva lot better equipped to deal with what they were going to face. Trevor was not going to let them down. Because he knew firsthand what lay in store for them. And it wasn't pretty flowers and weekend getaways.

Best he keep his mind on the job at hand himself.

THE FLOWERS were wilting. Christy knew she had to throw them away, but she stared at them instead, at the card still tucked amongst the brown-edged petals. "So much for the thunder, huh?" she muttered, reaching for the vase.

The phone rang, saving her once again. At least this time her heart didn't pick up pace, foolishly hoping there would be a deep voice on the other end. At least she wasn't being that pathetic.

"Hey there," said Viv when she answered. "Did

you just get off shift? I thought you were home today."

"I pulled a double. Dave and his girlfriend were having some problems, so I—"

"Came riding to the rescue," Viv said. "Why am I not surprised?"

"I'm hardly Mother Teresa," Christy replied dryly. "Plus, I could use the extra money for my renovations. My floors look great, but now I need to overhaul the cabinets. And when I can finally sit in my own kitchen without gagging, I'm going to start on the bathrooms. Please tell me they've outlawed avocado green. I mean, it's bad enough the toilet and sink look like baby puke, but the tub? What twisted mind thought that was a good idea?"

Vivian just laughed, she'd heard this rant many times since Christy moved into her condo six months earlier. "You know you love that old place and can't wait to make every little corner of it your own."

Christy looked around and once again felt the thrill of ownership. "Well, after that apartment I was renting, I'd be thankful for anything. But you're right. This place is special." She'd spent two years looking for the right place. She'd found plenty of them, but none in her price range. Then an apartment building closer to the renovated downtown area had gone condo. One of her co-workers had given her a heads up the day the units went on sale and she snagged her choice. There had been no haggling since the phone calls had come pouring in, so it had cost her, but it had been worth it.

So what if it took a few years to turn it into the place she knew it could be when she closed her eyes and imagined the finished product? She was actually sort of enjoying the process. Claiming the two-bedroom loft and blowing all her savings had been the easy part. Turning the place into a home—her home—was harder, but incredibly rewarding.

She sighed as her gaze fell on the flowers again.

"You'll get it all done," Viv said, misunderstanding the sigh. "We all know patience isn't your strong suit."

Christy could take the out and let Viv believe she was simply impatient about the renovations, but she realized she needed to talk. "It's not the condo. It's...it's Trevor."

"He'll call. Any man who sends flowers like that is going to call."

"It's been six days, Viv. I have to throw the flowers away."

"Oh, sweetie," Viv said, obviously hearing the disappointment in her voice. "Maybe you're right and he just doesn't know where to call."

"He knows where I work."

"And he knows you're in ICU. Maybe he doesn't want to disturb you."

Christy had told herself that, along with every other excuse she could think of.

"You know, there is a solution here."

"I'm not calling him, Viv. Besides, I have no idea

where he lives. He's starting his own business, but I don't know the name of it."

"Mike will know. He and Kate get home tomorrow from their honeymoon."

"No. The only talk you'll be having with Kate is listening to her apologize about her meddling."

"I'm not mad at her anymore. We'll clear it up, though," she added, cutting off Christy's lecture. "Besides—" she went on "—if she hadn't meddled, you'd never have met Trevor in the first place."

"I'm beginning to think that would have been better. At least I could keep my mind on work and not on—"

When the pause went on several moments, Viv just laughed. "Yeah, I'm not blind. I know what your mind's on. Mine would be, too. Let me get his number from Kate."

"I'm not chasing after him, Viv. If he wanted to see me, he'd find me. He was in special ops. Certainly he could find one woman in Richmond. If he wanted to."

"Calling him is not chasing. What's the difference between him calling you and you calling him?"

"When a man goes after a woman, it's romantic and dashing. When a woman does it, it's pathetic and desperate."

"I can't believe you said that."

Christy laughed. "Neither can I. So much for being the millennium woman."

"The what?"

"Never mind. But I'm still not calling him."

"You said he was starting a business. He's probably just caught up in that. Any man who sent flowers and that card would enjoy hearing from the woman he sent them to."

"Viv—"

"Christy," she shot right back.

"So tell me about lunch with Eric," Christy said instead. "This is five meals in six days. How much longer is he going to be here?"

"Not that you're in a hurry to get him on that plane or anything," Viv said with a laugh.

But Christy heard the thread of sadness. "It's soon, isn't it?" she asked gently.

"Another week."

Christy knew Viv and Eric had gone through a lot of painful revelations this week—some cathartic, some healing, some hurtful. But it had remained platonic throughout. Not so much as a kiss or even a hug, according to Viv. She hadn't said where it was all heading, either, and Christy hadn't pushed. Not too hard anyway.

"I'm—I don't know what to say," Christy said quietly.

"Say you'll call Trevor."

Christy laughed. "Boy, if anyone shouldn't be pushing someone into a relationship, you'd think it would be you."

"I push because I care," she said, laughing, too. "And I told you before, when it's the right one, it's worth the risk."

"Even after this week, you feel that way?"

"More than ever."

Christy didn't know what to make of that and was afraid to ask. "I don't know that Trevor is the right anything."

"Name me one man who, after meeting him once, has dominated your every thought the way Trevor has."

"Okay, okay. Point taken. But—"

"But why not find out? How else will you ever know?"

Christy sighed. "When are you seeing Eric again?"

"After my shift tomorrow. I have Tuesday off."

"Sounds potentially..."

"Interesting," Viv finished.

"Yeah."

After a slight pause, Viv said, "Stop worrying about me, Christy. I'm doing okay. I'm learning a lot about him. About us. But mostly I'm learning a lot about myself. I guess we never stop."

Thinking about the turmoil her thoughts and emotions had been in all week, just from one encounter with Trevor, she had to agree. "I guess not."

"So I'm getting Trevor's number. You can do with it what you want." She hung up before Christy could yell at her.

Instead she hung up the phone and picked up the vase. The card fell to the counter. "The thunder wasn't all outside the cabin." It said.

She thought about the way he'd looked at her, the

way he'd laughed with her. The way he'd kissed her. He was right; there had been thunder.

"So," she whispered, toying with the card. "What are you going to do about it, Millennium Woman?"

10

HE SHOULD HAVE left earlier. The rain was coming down in a torrent, sounding like heavy artillery firing on the warehouse roof. He could be tucked snug in his hotel room, but no, he'd stayed to install more training equipment. Then somehow he'd found himself testing out the padded dummy, which had turned into an hour's-long personal workout. Not that he was frustrated or anything.

He wiped the sweat off his forehead and tried to ignore the thrumming of rain on metal. One week to go and everything was moving along better than he'd hoped.

So why was it, after putting in another eighteen-hour day, with a million things to think about, worry over, plan for, all he could think about was Christy? He put another move on the dummy, then another, then another, until finally he swore and spun away.

He needed to call her. Talk to her. Maybe see her. Put that whole weekend back in perspective. "It was one kiss, for God's sake," he told himself. And not for the first time. Or even the tenth.

He propped his hands on his hips, a sheen of

sweat coating his face, chest and arms. The very idea of seeing her again, hearing her laugh, tasting her smile...well, it wasn't helping him cool down.

He scooped up his keys and the shirt he'd ripped off an hour ago. Maybe the walk to his car in the downpour would be the cold shower he so badly needed, but even as he let himself out the side door and locked everything up, he knew there was only one solution to his problem. Was it too late to call her now?

A deep rumble filled the night sky, making him pause as the rain soaked him the rest of the way. Then the sky split open over his head as a bolt of lightning shot across the sky, ripping it in two. His thoughts went immediately to Christy as he jogged the rest of the way to the used SUV he'd bought two days before and climbed inside. The windows fogged instantly with the dampness and heat radiating off his body. Another rumble vibrated the air.

He snagged his cell phone from the clip on his belt, then started the truck. It was only nine. He dialed in the number he'd memorized but had never used. He sat there, staring at it, finger hovering over the Call button, as another rumble vibrated the humid night air. "Just do it."

He didn't even know if she was working tonight. In a way, he hoped she was. She wouldn't hear the thunder as much inside the hospital and would be too busy to worry about it. And if she didn't pick up, he could just hang up and no one would be the wiser. His heart began to hammer inside his chest; he knew he wanted her to be home.

But just as he went to punch the Call button, it startled him by ringing. The incoming number flashed on the screen. It was the same one he'd almost dialed. A wide grin split his face. "Trevor's Thunder and Lightning Distraction Service," he said, more energized than he'd been in days.

She laughed. That's all it took and his body went rock hard. *Oh, yeah, just call her and put things in perspective.* Well, things were in perspective all right. He wanted her. Now. Tonight. All day tomorrow. Maybe even the next day. After that who knew and who cared?

"I told you to beware what you offered," she said.

"And I told you I never make offers I'm not willing to fulfill." He leaned back in his seat, heedless of the fact that he was drenched and starting to get a little chilly with the fan blowing. "You doing okay with the storm?"

There was a pause, then a dry laugh. "I'm not a complete neurotic mess you know."

"We all have our neuroses. Ask me how I feel about snakes sometime."

She chuckled and he could almost feel her relax. "Okay, Indiana McQuillen, I'll do that."

He shifted the phone to the other hand. "So you didn't call for a little...distraction?"

"I, uh..." She laughed. "Have no idea how to answer that one," she finished.

"Are you on shift tonight?"

"No. I'm off tonight and tomorrow. I don't go back until Tuesday."

"Want some company?" The question was out before he could think better of it. But, dammit, he wanted to see her. Hearing her wasn't enough. "We can meet somewhere if you'd like," he offered, shamelessly praying she would say no. He wanted her alone, all to himself. The power of that need should have had him backing off. But the past week hadn't put her further from his mind. In fact, it had done the exact opposite. One laugh and he realized he felt as if he'd been left in the desert to starve for six days. It made no sense, but right at the moment he didn't care.

"I might not be neurotic, but I'm not really up for going out in this mess. Would you—do you want to come here? I know it's late," she added. "Maybe some coffee?"

"Like the kind Viv makes?"

"I might be able to help you out there."

"Just tell me where and when," he said immediately.

"Bribed with Irish whiskey," she said on a laugh. "I've never tried that approach."

"I'm not coming for the whiskey."

There was a pause, then, "Oh."

A delicious sort of tension wound its way through him. He grinned in the darkness. "I like it when you get all tongue-tied. Or should I say, I like it when I make you all tongue-tied."

"Yes, well. Okay."

He didn't know whether to laugh or groan. Damn, but he wanted her. "Give me directions, Christy."

Her voice was definitely rougher as she told him. "Think you can find the right woman in the right be—uh, house, this time?"

Oh, that little slip did nothing to ease the growing pressure that was making his jeans tighter by the second. "I'm beginning to think I did pretty well last time."

She laughed at that. "Sleep deprivation aside, so am I."

"I'll be there in about twenty minutes."

"Where are you anyway? Viv, uh, got your number from Mike's folks. I wasn't sure if it was your home or..."

"It's my cell phone, which is both home and business for the time being until I get my phone lines put in. I'm in my truck, outside my warehouse."

"Your warehouse? I thought you said you were opening a training facility."

"I am. I'll have to bring you out here sometime, give you the tour. It's not much, but it's functional. Or will be when my first class starts next week."

"Next week? Wow, you work fast."

Thinking of where they'd ended up in that kitchen a week ago, he could hardly disagree. There was another pause and he smiled, knowing she'd just put the same thoughts together. "When I want something, I usually don't let much stand in my way of getting it."

She had to clear her throat. He had to curl his hands against the need to be touching her, right now.

"You've been putting in long hours. I probably shouldn't have called—"

"You put in long hours, too." He'd already put his truck into gear and was pulling out of the lot as he continued talking. "I want to see you, Christy. In fact, when I heard the thunder, I was going to call you."

"So, this is about the storm? Because I can handle—"

"Oh, I'm well aware that you can handle just about anything. The storm was just an excuse to do what I've been trying not to do all week."

"Why were you trying not to?"

He cursed himself for saying that. *Real smooth, McQuillen.* "All those long hours we both work. With everything going on here, I figured I should focus on one thing at a time. Problem is...I can't get you out of my mind."

"So tonight is...what?"

"Tonight is...finding out." He cleared his suddenly tight throat. "Finding out if we should think about making some time. For each other." There was a long pause and he wanted to smack himself. It wasn't like him to be this pushy. Okay, so it was exactly like him to be pushy, but not where women were concerned. Hell, it wasn't like him to want to move things forward period where women were concerned.

But with her there was a sense of urgency, this sense of time he could be spending with her that he wasn't, which felt like time wasted. "Christy, I'm—"

"Thinking about the thunder that's not outside?" she said tentatively.

"Yeah," he said roughly.

There was a pause, then, "So am I."

"Ten minutes," he told her as another bolt of lightning illuminated the night. "And forget about the whiskey."

She laughed and disconnected the call.

CHRISTY'S PALMS were sweating and it had nothing whatsoever to do with the summer storm raging outside. She had a pretty good storm raging inside, thank-you very much. She'd called. He was coming over. Viv would be so proud of her. Except now what in the hell did she do?

The knock at the door made her jump. It was then she realized she was still in her uniform, her hair was pinned back out of the way with little plastic clips and what little makeup she wore had long since worn off. She made a face at herself as she caught her reflection in the tiny hall mirror. Apparently she was doomed to never be at her best when she was around him. One look at her and he'd be begging for that Irish coffee, double on the whiskey please.

"Christy?"

Thunder shook the windowpanes and insecurity

shook her. He was right on the other side of that door. The man who'd sent her those flowers. The man she'd dreamed about. Hot, sweaty dreams that always left her achy and wanting. Right on the other side of that door.

She was going to kill Viv.

She slid the chain with clumsy fingers and unlocked the door, opening it a crack. Dear Lord. He was even better than in her dreams. And big. She'd known that, but the way he filled her doorway, all damp clothes and—and...raw masculinity... Well, it took what was left of her breath away. His short hair was plastered to his head, making the rugged angles of his cheeks and jaw stand out in sharp relief. And all of it made his eyes so luminous that once she looked into them, she couldn't look away.

"Hi," she managed.

"Hi," he said, his own voice a bit rough.

"You found me."

He grinned and her knees dipped. "Yes, ma'am."

"I—I didn't have a chance to change. I pulled an extra shift today and—"

He laughed and motioned to himself. "I hardly think you have to apologize for your appearance."

Yeah, she thought, *but you look sexy all soaking wet like that.* Then she realized she was keeping him standing, dripping in the hallway. "Come on in," she said, opening the door and stepping back, but when he moved inside there didn't seem to be enough room for the two of them.

He stopped, trapping her between him and the door. "I'm going to get you all wet."

God, I hope so, she thought feverishly.

"I should have gone to the hotel and changed first." He grinned again. "But I was sort of in a hurry."

"Yeah. Hurry," she repeated, dazed by how close he was, so close he could touch her. *Please touch me.*

As if he'd read her mind, he traced a finger along her cheek and she trembled as a shaky breath slid from between her lips.

"I missed you," he said quietly. One by one, he plucked the plastic clips from her hair. Then he sunk his fingers into her hair and shook it loose, holding her head as he lowered his own. "I should never have waited. Now I'm half starved for this."

"Starved," she agreed, and lifted her mouth to his.

It was better than any dream, better even than the kiss in Viv's kitchen. She was hungry, so hungry. And so was he. Yet he didn't devour, though there was a distinct part of her that would have enjoyed it if he had. Instead he kissed her slowly, thoroughly, continually, as if he was indeed starved and was going to get his fill, all in one kiss. She braced her hands on his chest as he backed her against the open door.

His wet shirt should have been cold and clammy. It wasn't. His chest beneath was warm, almost hot to the touch. She was surprised steam wasn't rising off of him.

"You—you shouldn't be in wet clothes," she said as he trailed kisses along her jaw and up to her temple.

"I was thinking the same thing," he said, carefully not getting his wet body too close to hers, which somehow only served to make the air between them even more erotically charged. He lifted his mouth from her skin, looking into her eyes. "I could go change."

"You could," she agreed, then tugged him the rest of the way inside.

He laughed and pulled her hard against him as he kicked the door shut behind him. "You'll get wet."

"I already am."

He groaned and pulled her more tightly into his arms. "Christy—"

"Did I really just say that?" she whispered against his hammering heart, laughing at herself.

He looked down at her. "I believe that was you, yes." He nipped at her nose, then playfully at the corners of her mouth, then kissed her eyes shut as she sighed and leaned more fully into him. "Do we need to stop this for coffee?" he asked roughly, his lips against her ear.

She shook her head, not wanting to do anything that would take him even one centimeter away from where he was at this moment.

"Do we need to stop this...for any other reason?"

She opened her eyes now and looked into his. The desire she saw there had her knees going wonky again. But it was the caring concern that touched her heart. If she said no to any more than this, he'd be a gentleman and not push her. But she didn't want to say no. It went against all her normal cautions, but with Trevor...she couldn't explain it. Thoughts of that soul-mate conversation flickered through her mind, but she shoved it aside and simply went with what she felt.

"No," she whispered. That fierce light almost engulfed his eyes the instant she uttered the word. Her pulse thundered, her body was already past needing any additional priming. "But—"

He was already moving to kiss her again, but he paused. "But?"

"I want—" Now she felt self-conscious. But this was important, this step with him. It wasn't casual, not to her, and she had to tell him that, now. Before. "I want you, this...I feel like I can't think straight until we—" She laughed even as she flushed.

"I know," he said, smiling. "I feel the same way." He pushed her hair back with his fingertips, then framed her face with his big hands. "It's more than just this, Christy. Or it can be."

She trembled. "Should it be more...before we... you know?"

"Does it feel that way to you?"

"It should. But it doesn't. I just wanted you to know that I don't usually—"

"I know," he said, pulling her closer until their lips almost touched. "I know." Then he kissed her, and this time there was something else there, woven in with the passion and the hunger. Something almost...reverent.

She pulled at his shirt. "Take this off." She'd meant to ask more politely, but it came out as a sort of growl.

Still kissing her, he trailed his hands down to her shoulders, then down her arms until her hands were in his. He placed them on the buttons. Against her lips, he murmured, "You take it off."

A shudder of pleasure went through her at the prospect of feeling his skin beneath her fingers. She was clumsy with her desire and it took her several tries with each button before she successfully freed it. Of course, his kisses didn't help her equilibrium any.

She struggled to push the wet fabric down his shoulders, but it got all bunched up on his biceps until he finally dragged it the rest of the way off. She pressed her hands to his chest, unable to resist direct contact with that wall of warm flesh.

He groaned and covered her hands with his. "Christy." It was all he could manage, but he released her hands and let her trail them over his chest as she wished.

Dear God, but he was stunning. His chest was hard, almost carved, his muscles all rigid and defined. She ran a long finger down the line bisecting his abs, when he finally shuddered and covered her hand, stopping her exploration just above the waistband of his jeans.

"Fair is fair," he said shakily. He let her hand go,

then lightly traced those long fingers along her waist, toying with the edges of her top. Only there weren't any buttons on hers. So he slowly lifted the hem, forcing her to put her arms over her head so he could slip it off. She shivered and felt a twinge or two of insecurity before recalling he'd seen her in nothing more than a skimpy tank top the first time they'd met. Still...this was different. This was—

The thought disappeared on a gasp as his warm mouth closed over her nipple through the cotton bra she wore. Her arms were still over her head, caught in the sleeves he still held as he dipped his head and took her other nipple.

He groaned, or maybe it was her. All she knew was that her legs were not going to keep her upright much longer if he insisted on— Dear Lord. Her knees buckled as he yanked off the top, then moved his hands down her arms, lowering them so he could slide her bra straps down over her shoulders, pulling the soft cotton down over her breasts, over her now fully hardened nipples. "Trevor," she rasped.

"So warm, so soft," he said, almost reverently.

"Can't...stand...up," she managed.

He laughed and went to swing her up into his arms. That galvanized her into action. She stumbled back, avoiding certain humiliation. She was not a small woman, in height or stature, and it was one thing for him to toss her over his shoulder like a sack of flour, or carry her all stiff and trussed-up like a Thanksgiving turkey, but quite another to scoop

her up all mushy and relaxed, a hundred and—
"Ooph!"

"Tabletop, couch or bed?" he asked, grinning down at her stunned expression.

He was strong, and hungry...and it was her he was going to devour. She shivered in delicious anticipation. "Bed. Loft. Upstairs." She gestured in the general direction of the open staircase that wound to the second-floor loft. But it was hard as she was pretty sure her eyes had rolled to the back of her head when he tucked her up higher so he could sample her nipples again.

That squeal was definitely hers. The delighted laughter was his. Dear God, couldn't he climb the damn stairs any faster?

The storm raged outside, but the one inside her was the only one commanding her attention at the moment. That and the one in his blue eyes. It was dim in her loft, with only scant illumination from the lamp in the living room below, but he found her bed with no problem. They were both panting, more with need than exertion, when he finally climbed onto the bed with her still in his arms...only to leave her there and quickly hop right back off again. Before she could question his sudden abandonment, he looked up and said, "Wet jeans."

"Oh. Right." *So hurry up and get them off*, she silently demanded. Then realized she was in her scrub bottoms as well and started to skim them down her hips. It gave her something to do instead of looking at him. Because all of a sudden looking at him completely naked seemed too overwhelming, too personal, too— She peeked. Then didn't look away.

The bottom half of him was as sculpted...and rigidly formed...as the top half. He was total perfection. And he was going to be all hers.

Her hands stilled on the drawstring of her pants. Yes, he'd seen her in her underwear, but he hadn't been thinking of her that way at that point. Now...

"Take off your pants, Christy."

"What?" She was staring...and not at her pants.

"Slide them down your hips for me."

He took a step closer to the bed. "Or would you like it if I did it for you?"

It wasn't a threat. It was an invitation. And he made it sound damn inviting, too. Oh the dilemma.

He kneeled onto the bed, ready for her and completely unashamed of it. "Let me see you."

She couldn't explain the sudden shyness. It really made no sense, considering he'd already seen almost all of her anyway. But he was so damn perfect...and she was so...not.

He bent down and put his hands over hers on the drawstrings. "I dream about you, Christy. Your warm skin, how your curves feel under my hands." He tugged at the string and her hands fell away. But as he slid them down her legs, his gaze stayed directly on hers. "But that's just part of it." He tossed away her pants and levered himself over her. "Your body is beautiful and lush enough to keep me aroused for hours, days..." He lowered his weight onto hers and they both gasped, then moaned at the contact. But before she could react, he looked directly into her eyes and said, "But it's hearing your laugh, seeing your smile, that got me this way in the first place. It's about all of you, Christy. You wanted this to be about more." He nudged between her legs and her hips lifted to his as naturally as if she had indeed been made just for him. He slowly pushed inside her. "And it is. A whole lot more."

11

TREVOR SHOOK, both with the impact the reality of his words had on him...and with the tight feel of her all around him, taking him in, so deeply, so surely. There was no going back, not with their bodies or anything else. He knew it, and looking down into her eyes as he began to move inside her, he saw she knew it, too.

He should be scared, terrified even. He'd avoided this very thing for so long. But he realized now that he hadn't avoided anything. It simply hadn't happened. Because there was no avoiding it when it did, indeed, happen.

Her hips rose to find him, meeting his thrusts. She gripped his arms and wrapped herself completely around him, body, heart and soul. He sunk into all that she offered...and did it willingly. It *was* scary, and even a bit terrifying...but only because it felt like home. There was no other way to describe it. He had searched the globe, coming back to the only place that had felt like home, and only now did he realize home wasn't a geographic location.

He thrust deeper, growling as he gave himself

completely over to the unbelievable wonder of his discovery. She met him, thrust for thrust.

"Trevor," she panted.

"I know," he said, and kept saying it as they both climbed higher and higher. She was thrashing beneath him now, her cries wild and uninhibited, shoving him right to the brink. He wanted to tell her, somehow make her understand what he was feeling, but it was all a jumble of want and need and his body was taking control.

He gripped her head and took her mouth, kissing her with everything he had inside of him, stunned at the depth of it. The force of his climax shuddered through him, eliciting a long, low growl. But he was rocked even further by the mystifying, yet certain knowledge that she was the one. Home would forever be wherever Christy Russell was.

Still trembling, he looked down into her face, pushing away the hair that clung damply to her heated skin, stroking her until she opened her eyes and looked at him. It awed him, this sense he had of the complete rightness of their being together. And it wasn't diminishing now that his body's needs had been sated. In fact...

He opened his mouth to tell her, find the words to make her understand...and realized he couldn't. She wanted more, yes, but this was so overwhelming, he wasn't sure she was ready for it. Hell, he wasn't sure he was ready for it!

If he tried to explain it all to her, she'd probably think he was insane and run screaming into the night. Major tactical error. No, he'd simply have to show her. Here in her bed. Out of bed. In the morning, the middle of the night...and all those times in between. Until she knew. Like he knew.

"What?" Her voice was barely more than a rasp.

He stroked his fingers down her cheek, feeling both immensely satisfied and antsy with anticipation of what was to come. "What what?" he asked, still toying with her hair.

She smiled, looking languorous and content. "That smile on your face. It's quite...predatory."

He grinned and kissed her. "Well, I'm feeling a bit...predatory."

"Are you?" She laughed when he pretended to pounce on her neck, then sighed as he slid his mouth to that tender spot on her shoulder. "How can you...after what we..." The rest was lost on a low moan of pleasure as he moved to the plump side of her breast. "You're still—" She inhaled sharply as he pulled her nipple between his lips and suckled it.

"I'm still," he said, moving his mouth across her stomach. "But you won't be. Move for me, Christy." He dipped his tongue into her and she bucked her hips hard off the bed. He moved his body to pin her down, grinned as he lost himself between her legs, pushing her right up to the edge...and then screaming right over it.

He kissed his way back up her still-shuddering body and pulled her into his arms. "Now I'm full."

For now, he thought, already planning how their morning might unfold.

Waking up next to her... He smiled at the thought, then paused, wondering if she'd even let him stay the night. *Might want to slow down here, McQuillen,* he schooled himself. One step at a time. But he didn't want to go slow. And they didn't seem to move step by step, more like leaps and bounds. He was fine with that.

He'd simply have to make sure she didn't want him to leave. If she wanted to sit up all night and talk, distract herself from the storm, fine. There were a lot of things they had to say to each other yet. If she wanted other sorts of distraction, well that was fine, too. Whatever it took.

She snuggled against his chest then, curling a leg over his and snaking her arm around his waist. He grinned in the darkness and pulled her closer. They would have to talk, but right now just feeling her falling asleep in his arms was pretty damn wonderful. The talking could wait. He tucked her head under his chin just as thunder shook the house and lightning lit up the room. She didn't even flinch.

"Sweet dreams, Christy," he whispered. Then he let himself drift off to sleep, a smile on his face.

SOMETHING WAS NIBBLING on her shoulder. Christy swatted it away, grumbled something, then tried to pull her pillow over her head. No alarms were going off so it wasn't time to get up yet. But her pillow was stuck or something.

She didn't want to open her eyes, so she tried to roll over and pull the covers over her head instead. Something big and hard and warm was in her way, however. She blinked her eyes against the morning light and felt around in front of her. Definitely hard, definitely big. And very warm.

"Morning."

She screamed. Okay, so it had come out as more of a muffled croak, but that didn't stop the adrenaline from pumping through her. She tried to fight off the covers and sit up, but something hard and very strong was holding her down.

"Christy," said the same deep voice. This was followed by a warm, very wonderful kiss on her shoulder.

She decided not to fight the warm, hard thing. It felt pretty good. She sunk back into her covers, sighing in pleasure as the warm kisses continued, moving along her neck to her jaw, then down to her earlobe. She snuggled more deeply against the warm thing. "Mmm," she murmured as the kisses moved along the shell of her ear.

"Good morning," he whispered, then pushed her hair out of the way so he could kiss her along the back of her neck.

She rolled on her stomach, thinking this pretty much beat the hell out of having to set half a dozen alarm clocks every morning. Why hadn't she thought of this solution sooner? She groaned as warm hands ran down along her back, then upward again, into her hair. Suddenly she was being rolled to her back and her eyes blinked open as warm lips found the side of her breast.

A blurry image of Trevor lifted his head and grinned at her. "You taste wonderful first thing in the morning."

"Hunph." She let her head flop back on the pillow, but moved rather quickly to hold his head where it was when he would have moved it away.

"Ah," he said teasingly. "Your morning verbal skills leave a bit to be desired, but you more than make up for that with sign language."

She grunted something that was supposed to sound like "Yes, sir," but his lips closed over her nipple just then and she found she really didn't care that much about clear diction.

He slid his body over hers as he moved to her other nipple, nudging her legs apart as he continued his most excellent morning wake-up routine. He lifted his head, and when she whimpered in protest and grabbed at his hips, he said, "Look at me, Christy."

She blinked her eyes open again. He filled her vision this time and so she kept her eyes open until he finally came into focus. "Hi," she said, smiling sleepily.

He pushed just a tiny bit inside her, and grinned when her hips jerked. "Hi."

"You are going to finish what you've started, right?" she asked, her voice all raspy. "Because I'm not up to homicide this morning. Besides, they frown on that in my line of work."

"Oh, I'm going to finish. I just wanted to make sure you were all the way with me."

"All the way," she said on a sigh. "All the way sounds really good right now."

"Like this?" He slid in partway and she clutched at him, groaning in pleasure.

"Something like that," she managed, fighting to keep her eyes open when they wanted to roll to the back of her head. "More. I want more."

"More?" He nudged a bit more. "Like this?"

"No." She hooked her ankle behind his and before he could read her intent, she flipped him onto his back, rolling with him. As soon as her body lifted over his, she sank fully down onto him, groaning in absolute ecstasy as she did so. "Like this," she said, bracing herself on his shoulders.

"Ah," he said, grinning up at her.

She moved on him, making him groan and squeeze his eyes shut as she continued to slide her body on his. "No," she said lustily. "That would be ahhhhh."

Trevor pulled her down, sinking his fingers into her hair so he could hold her head while he kissed her. Deep, soul kisses that reached even further into her than his body was. She felt fully penetrated by him, every part of her, mind, body and soul. And she didn't want it to end. She only wanted to penetrate him just as fully.

He locked his ankles over hers and pulled her taut on top of him, continuing to thrust up into her with strong, deep strokes. She moved his hands and pinned them to the bed, dipping down to kiss him where she wanted, how she wanted, for as long as she wanted even as he continued his assault on her from below. They each claimed the other, even as they were claimed by the other. She thought it was the perfect union.

She climbed higher and higher toward release, wishing she could stave it off, but relishing the intensity she knew awaited her when she peaked.

"Christy," he said hoarsely.

She felt him gather beneath her, his hips moving faster and faster. "Trevor," she said gently. Dipping her head down, she took his mouth in a tender kiss that was totally at odds with the ferocity of their coupling.

He came the instant her lips touched his, spiking her over the top an instant later. She felt his deep-groaning release vibrate against her lips as their kiss continued long after their climaxes subsided.

He shifted them to their sides and pulled her close. "I could kiss you for hours," he said.

"Haven't you been?" she said, blinking up at him.

He smiled. "It feels like I've only just started."

Something blossomed inside her chest then. It felt a whole lot like her heart. Only it couldn't be, because that would mean she was falling in love with him. And she wasn't ready for that yet. She couldn't be. Too risky.

She had a fleeting thought of Viv and what she was going through. She didn't want to be in a position to worry about those kinds of risks, that potential for pain. And yet, when she looked into the blue eyes gazing back at her right now...she honestly didn't want to be anywhere else on the planet.

"Wheels are turning in there," he said.

"I might take a while to wake up, but when I do—" She paused to playfully push at him when he rolled his eyes.

"Hey," he said, laughing, "I'm not the one with a dozen alarm clocks all over my bedroom."

"There's only six," she said primly. "And, as I was saying before being so rudely interrupted—" She was interrupted again, this time by a fast, deep kiss that left her breathless.

"You were saying?"

"I have no idea."

"Works every time."

She smacked at him, but he snagged her hand in midswing and tugged her back on top of him. She flipped him back. He grabbed a pillow, she grabbed him...and a pillow fight wrestling match ensued that ended with them both on the floor in a tangle of bedclothes and each other.

They were both laughing so hard neither one of them could speak. Christy was sprawled helplessly across his chest, thinking this was the absolute best morning of her life. She was a heartbeat away from telling him that, but stopped herself. Those sorts of declarations probably weren't a good idea. Not yet, anyway. He was here and not in any hurry to leave apparently. For now, that was enough. She had to take this one step at a time.

Now if only she could just find a way to make her heart understand the logic of that plan.

"Are you a big-breakfast person?" Trevor asked her as he disentangled himself from the twisted sheets.

"Not normally, no."

"Today?"

She gave him a look. "Ravenous."

He winked at her. "I meant for food."

"That, too."

Laughing, he caught her off guard and wrapped her in the sheet before she knew what he was about, then scooped her up ridiculously easily and plopped her on the bed. "Shower or bath?"

"Depends," she tossed back. "Solo or with company?"

"Depends. Breakfast now? Or breakfast later?"

She grinned. "Later. Shower with company, please. We wouldn't both fit in the tub."

"Is that a dare?" he asked, leaning over her, totally unselfconscious about his nudity.

Which was a good thing, she thought, since she found she'd become totally unselfconscious about looking at him naked. "It could be," she responded.

"If I win and we both fit?"

"Then I'd say we're probably both going to be winners," she answered with a laugh. "Or needing the services of my emergency-room staff."

He scooped her up again. "I think we can manage this without their help." He carried her to the adjoining bathroom. "When did you say you had to be back at work?"

"Not till tomorrow afternoon."

He grinned and kissed her. "Good. We just might be done by then." He kicked the door shut behind them.

TREVOR UNLOCKED the warehouse door, then reached in to flick on the lights. "This is the training center. The other building is offices and classrooms. Or will be. I don't have all the rooms set up yet, just enough to start my first class next weekend."

Christy walked inside and looked all around. "I can't believe you've gotten all this done since the wedding."

Trevor went past her and flicked on the rest of the lights. "Well, I bought the land and the buildings over a year ago. I've been slowly working on it, ordering stuff in, planning. Every chance I got to fly back anyway. The rest I did long-distance."

She turned in a slow circle. "Very impressive." She stopped in front of him. "I think it's wonderful what you're doing, even if the whole idea is a bit intimidating."

Her praise meant a lot to him. "It's necessary," he said. "We need more facilities like this one."

"Will you have to go overseas with your students? Do any training over there?"

He looked into her eyes. She was worried. About him. It felt good, even though he didn't want her to. He stepped closer and framed her face with his hands. "I've been in life-and-death situations many times, you know."

She nodded, started to say something, then stopped.

His pulse picked up speed. "What?"

"Nothing. You're right. You're trained to handle this kind of thing. It's just—" She stopped, then shrugged.

"Just what? You don't like the idea of me going back overseas, putting myself in situations like that again?"

"I don't have any right to make that kind of statement."

"Sure you do. It's a feeling. You have a right to feel." He tugged her closer when she would have pulled away. "And if it makes you feel any better, I like it that you feel that way."

She looked up at him. "So...are you? Going back, I mean?"

He smiled and shook his head. "That's why I got out. I want to help, but I'm done with traipsing around the world. I want..." He shook his head then, knowing he couldn't tell her all the things he wanted, especially all the things he wanted when he looked at her. She wasn't ready to hear that yet, he knew. "I want friends, stability. I want to build a life." *With you.* "I want to be able to start friendships, relationships I know I'll be there to continue, to build on." He tipped her chin. "So, no, no more traveling for me. I'm home to stay." He kissed her, silently telling her all the things he couldn't say out loud. Not yet. But soon. If he was very lucky and didn't screw this up.

She leaned into him, kissing him back, and he thought he could stand here, just like this, forever.

She finally pulled away, smiling at him, then wandering off to look at the various equipment. "So, this is where you grew up, then? Richmond?"

"Only partly. I was a military brat. With my dad." She turned then and he knew what she was thinking. "My mom died when I was a baby."

"That must have been hard on your dad."

"It was. I came to live with my grandmother. Here. Until I was old enough for school. Then my dad decided I should be with him. After that it was two years here, two years there." He shrugged. "I came back as often as I could to visit her. So I guess this is as close to a regular home as I've had."

He'd said it matter-of-factly, which is how he felt about it now. He knew Christy had grown up without a father, so she probably understood better than anyone. She proved she did when she didn't sigh in pity or make sad noises, which was exactly why he didn't usually bring it up with the women he dated. But he wanted her to know, to understand who he was, where he'd come from.

She went back to looking at the equipment. "No sisters, brothers?"

Now he smiled. She asked casually enough, but he sensed she was dying of curiosity to know him better. That pleased him more than she could know. It should have felt odd, after all the years of automatically deflecting conversation away from himself. But it didn't. In fact, it felt...necessary. "My dad never remarried. He was dedicated to the service. He passed away a couple of years ago. Cancer."

She turned to him again, this time there was sadness in her eyes. "I'm sorry." She walked over to him. "I know how hard that is."

"And you were just a kid."

"Yeah, but I had my mom. Still do. And even though she can make me nuts, I can't imagine not knowing she's out there somewhere, making some man nuts, too." She smiled when he laughed.

"I'd love to meet her," he said.

Christy raised her eyebrows in surprise, but just said, "Be careful what you wish for."

"I believe we've discussed that before."

She laughed. "Yeah, well, this time you might have bitten off more than you can chew."

"If she gave birth to you, I'm sure I'll adore her."

Christy paused then, and looked at him, but laughed as if he were joking.

"Does she visit often?" he asked.

"You're going to push this, aren't you? And thankfully, no," she added, before he could respond. She rolled her eyes and, more to herself than him, said, "God, I can only imagine what she'd say if she met you."

"What is that supposed to mean?"

Christy spun away from him then, clearly wishing she'd kept the thought to herself. "Nothing. She's just pushy, is all. When she's not matching herself up, she's trying to match me up." She smiled ruefully. "Just be thankful she's in Florida at the moment. Trust me, your life is more peaceful that way."

"I don't know," he said, walking back over to her. "I sort of like the uproar my life has become since you've come into it."

"Uproar?"

He closed the remaining distance between them. "Thunder. Lots of thunder." He bent down and kissed her. "I'm beginning to love storms."

She kissed him back, then pulled from his arms and wandered off into the cavernous warehouse. "So, tell me what you do with all this stuff."

Trevor wanted to push further, but he sensed he'd pushed hard enough for now. They had all day together...and tonight, too, if he was lucky. He felt as if he'd been granted the best furlough of his life. He wasn't about to do anything that would end it prematurely.

12

"YOU'RE WHAT?" Christy slumped back against the cafeteria seat. "You can't be serious."

Viv smiled and nodded. "I know you don't understand. But it's what I want."

"So he wins. After all this, he comes home for a couple weeks—"

"It's been a month. And it wasn't easy for him to postpone going back. In fact, it cost him plenty."

"So because he adds a few more weeks, this makes things even?"

"It's not about being even. I don't want to be without him anymore, Christy." Viv reached for her hand. "I know you think I'm giving in, but it's not like that. Things between us have changed. Both of us have changed."

"You're walking away from your home, your family, friends and career. He gets his career and you, without sacrificing anything. How is that a change?"

"Because now I realize he's worth it."

"But you're not? Why isn't he giving up his career?" Christy persisted. "Why isn't he coming back here to be with you?"

Viv only grew more determined. "What we had together was more important than any job, or even sticking by my family." She smiled then. "No offense, as much as I value what we share, but you don't keep me warm at night. And as much as my family means to me, I want to build my own family. If I have to go to Sweden to do that, then I'm willing to try."

Christy sat back. "You're really serious about this, aren't you?"

"I love him, I miss him. I never got over him leaving and I don't want him to leave again. If that makes me a spineless fool, then so be it. At least I'll be a happy spineless fool."

"You're not spineless. And I want you to be happy," Christy said softly. "I've always wanted that." She shook her head, still unable to take it all in. "It's just you went through so much and I'm afraid—"

"I know," Viv said softly. "I know, and I can't tell you how much it means to me that you care so deeply. I love you, too."

Christy felt her eyes well up.

"If it makes you feel any better, we're not rushing off to get remarried or anything. Not yet. We really want to make this work, we want a future with each other, but we need to make sure we can work out the basics first, including me transplanting my whole life to a foreign country. I've agreed to a six-month trial run, then we'll go from there."

"Six months?" Christy felt a little bit of relief.

"I've taken leave here and I know I'll lose some benefits and my place on the food chain, but it's a price I'm willing to pay. Eric tells me I'll love Sweden and maybe I will. I plan to go and try my best. He already looked into the nursing situation there and it might be more promising than I thought. He says English is spoken most everywhere. And, if I just don't like it, he'll look into trying to relocate back here." She gripped Christy's hand. "I can't ask for much more than that. We want to be together. We are both willing to work at it when things get rough, instead of running away. You know we were great together and miserable apart. I meant what I said about building a family of my own. If we can make this work, we both want to start a family. I want that, Christy. With him."

Stunned, Christy just sat there, then shoved her chair back so she could lean across the table and hug her friend. "Oh, Viv, sweetie, I hope everything works out for you." She sat back down. "I mean that, you know. I worry, but I have to honestly say that I haven't seen you this happy and hopeful for a long time." She sniffled and wiped at her eyes. "But you're not going to rush into the family part, are you? I mean, you want to make sure—"

Viv laughed. "Yes, Mom. We're going to make sure we've worked out everything else first."

"Okay, then." She smiled. "I guess you're allowed." She waved a finger. "But only if I get to be godmother. Years from now. When the time is right."

Vivian hugged her again. "Promise. Not about the years, though."

Christy just nodded, trying to come to terms with the fact that Viv was really going to do this. "I can't believe you're going to leave me." She laughed through a fresh wash of tears. "Who am I going to rant about work to? Who am I going to dish about all the good gossip with?"

"There is e-mail in Sweden, you know."

"When are you going?" she asked, blotting her now-ruined mascara with a cafeteria napkin.

"I have to look into renting out my place and take care of a few other things. My family for one."

Christy made a face, but squeezed Viv's hand. "I'm sure they'll support you if they know it's what you really want. And I know you want this, Viv. I do." She hugged her friend again. "Of course, if he hurts you again, the world won't be big enough for him to find a hiding place."

Vivian laughed, then sniffled herself. "I'll tell him."

Another thought popped into Christy's head. "Hey, I might be able to help you out on the rental. With all the preparations for that first class, Trevor never had time to look for a place. Now he's got another class already set up and he's scrambling to finish the other classrooms. He has no time to spend hunting for a place."

Vivian wiggled her eyebrows. "I thought he was pretty much staying with you."

Christy swatted at her, but couldn't stop the smile

from spreading across her face. "Yeah, well, it's been convenient is all."

"Uh-huh," Viv said, a knowing look on her face. "I've heard it does help a person's sex life when you're actually in the same bed." She grinned. "Now you know the real reason I'm going to Sweden."

They both laughed.

"I guess I'll have to fly back for the wedding, huh?" Viv teased. "You two are almost inseparable, which is quite a feat with your work schedules."

Christy held up her hands. "Whoa, now. Hold your horses. We're just dating. Having fun. Nothing serious."

"Right. I've seen the way he looks at you, Christy. And, you might not want to hear it, but you look at him the same way. You two are perfect together."

Christy didn't respond right away. She'd been trying very hard not to think of the future, of long-term things. Too scary. "I'm just enjoying things as they come, Viv. I don't have time to think about the rest."

"You don't want to think about the rest."

"Same thing."

"Hardly. I know we've been all caught up in my latest drama, but I've been paying attention even if you haven't. You can't tell me you aren't absolutely head over heels about this guy. And what's not to love? He's intelligent, gorgeous and knows just how to handle you."

Christy bristled. "*Handle* me?"

Viv didn't even blink. "Totally. You're your own person, you've got your own ideas about things. That intimidates most men. Not Trevor. He's got you pegged. He knows you're tough on the outside and all soft and squishy on the inside. And he likes who you are." She grinned. "Smart guy, in my book." Then she leaned forward and whispered, "But if makes you feel any better, you've got him just as wrapped around that little finger of yours."

"We're just dating, Viv," she said stubbornly.

"You keep telling yourself that. Just remember I told you so when he proposes."

Christy laughed, or tried to. It was hard, what with her throat suddenly constricting and all. "Proposes?" she croaked. "He just moved here, Viv. He's starting up a business. He's got a ton of things on his mind. The last thing he wants to do is—"

"Settle down? Gee, no, doesn't sound like that's what he's doing at all. Uh-uh." Vivian just laughed when Christy tried to protest again, then turned serious when Christy didn't laugh with her. "What are you afraid of?"

Christy wasn't sure how to answer that, but she and Viv had always been blunt with each other. "I'm afraid of ending up where you were eighteen months ago. Where my mother ends up every couple of years, though in her case, I will admit she doesn't usually seem all that broken up about it. But that seems even worse to me, somehow—not even caring enough in the first place to be upset when it doesn't work out."

"Meaning you care enough about Trevor that if it didn't work out, you'd be hurt?"

Christy started to object, then sighed and gave in. "Yes. Yes, if I decided to get serious about him, about this relationship...it would hurt if it ended. Badly."

Viv clapped and smiled. "I knew it!"

"You have a twisted sense of humor. Has anyone ever told you that?"

"Don't you see? You're already serious. I knew it." She grabbed both of Christy's hands. "That's a good thing, believe it or not."

"I'm not so sure," Christy grumbled.

Viv gave her a considering look. "Okay then, maybe you should spare him and walk away now."

"What?" The flash of pain she felt at even the mention of walking away from Trevor should have been warning enough that Viv had a point. Christy didn't want to think about it. But her friend wasn't having any of it.

"See. Just the idea of walking away already hurts. You love him, Christy. Or you're well on your way. Why don't you just go ahead and fall the rest of the way? Enjoy it, for God's sake. This is the wonderful part, you dork."

"Don't you have a plane to Sweden to catch?" Christy muttered.

Viv ignored her. "Life is full of pitfalls and disappointments. If I learned anything, it's that you can hide away from life hoping to miss the bad stuff, but then you'll miss out on all the good stuff. So what's the point in being here? There's pleasure and joy, too, you know."

"I wasn't exactly miserable before I met Trevor, you know. I have a life."

"I know. But now you have him in it, too. And you've found there can be even more joy and pleasure in sharing your ups and downs with someone else."

Christy smiled. "That's what I have you for." But Viv wasn't going to let it go. "Okay, so you're right. You don't give me great sex. He is good for that."

Viv gave her another look. "Is that all it is? Great sex?"

Christy wanted to say yes, but she couldn't lie. Not to Viv. "No. It's more."

"You know what I think?"

Christy's mouth quirked. "No, Dr. Viv, why don't you tell me?"

Viv leaned back and folded her arms. "I think you're subconsciously afraid of being abandoned. Which is sort of what your dad did, though obviously not on purpose." She raised a hand to stave off Christy's rebuttal. "Hear me out. Then there are all the men in your mom's life. Not one is still around."

"Mom is hardly a good example. I mean, even I know she doesn't take them seriously enough to—"

"I said *sub*consciously. I know you understand all this rationally, in your head. But here—" she tapped her heart "—here I think you haven't quite convinced yourself that if you let someone close, in the end, they're going to abandon you, too. Why else does every man you date become more of a buddy than a lover?"

"Because I'm not a perfect size four, blond, with perky boobs?"

"Because it's safer being a pal than a lover, that's why. And I'm to blame here, too. I'm your best friend and it's not helping this subconscious manifestation of yours witnessing my trials and tribulations with Eric."

"Oh, great, now I'm having subconscious manifestations. Do I need an exorcist or an exterminator? Sheesh, Viv."

Viv propped her elbows on the table. "Okay, then. Tell me why you're not totally blissed out over having what is probably the best time of your life with Trevor? What's holding you back?"

Christy wanted to give it right back to her, to tell her in no uncertain terms that her theory was a crock of bull hockey. But the words weren't there. She fiddled with her fork. "I'm just— He's just— It's..." She shrugged, then dropped her chin to her chest. "God, maybe you're right and I'm a closet basket case." She took a deep breath and looked up. "It scares me how much I enjoy being with him, Viv. I've never felt anything like this in my life. I want more, but I'm afraid of reaching for it. I'm afraid of what will happen if I reach and it's not there. Or worse, I grab hold, only to have it yank itself free."

"Remember what I said at the cabin? You asked me if it was worth the risk. Let me ask you something. Would you give back what you've already had with him for the safety of never having felt it?"

"No," Christy said, the swiftness and certainty of her response a sort of epiphany of its own.

Viv looked at her friend. "Then don't be so worried about the possibility of pain that you miss out on all the joy. It *is* worth the risk, Christy."

CHRISTY WATCHED Trevor towel off his truck. She decided there was something inherently erotic about watching a half-naked man wash his vehicle. She leaned back against her already-sparkling car and sipped at her soda. Her body twitched as he slowly rubbed the towel along the shiny metal dips and curves. Oh, yeah, she thought, admiring the play of muscles along his shoulders, she could make this a weekly routine, no problem.

In fact, at the moment, she thought she could easily spend her whole life watching him with that towel. He turned that moment and caught her staring.

He winked and swatted her bare calves with the towel. "I'm almost done here."

"Don't hurry on my account," she said.

He lifted his eyebrows, but caught on to the focus of her attention quickly. With a leering smile, he continued drying the truck, but in such an overtly sexual manner, she found herself laughing. And getting turned on. Trevor did things like that to her.

It's worth the risk. Viv's words came back to her, as they had almost every day since their little talk two weeks before. She'd thought about it a lot. All of it. And she'd had to admit that perhaps her best friend knew her better than she knew herself. But understanding, or trying to, didn't automatically make the fears go away.

Because Viv was right about another thing, too. Christy was falling for Trevor. Hard. And with frightening swiftness. She didn't want to pull back, but at the same time, she couldn't help but want to freeze things at this moment. When it was fun and exciting and new. When the risk seemed miles away because it was all fresh and the anticipation was still at its peak.

"You're thinking again."

"Silly me," she said dryly, liking how his teasing smile made her feel. "If I'm not careful, I slip and do that from time to time."

Trevor was leaning back against his now-gleaming truck, studying her in that disconcerting way he had. The way that told her he had, indeed, come to know her very well. In fact, she couldn't really remember a time when he didn't know her well. It was as if they were two puzzle pieces who had finally been put together. The fit was immediate and perfect.

Something had to be wrong with that picture. It couldn't be that easy. Could it?

He pushed away and walked up to her, all damp and sweaty and beautiful. "Want to talk about it?"

"Talk about what?" she said, tracing patterns on his chest with her fingers, hoping to distract him.

"About whatever it is that's bothering you. Is it Viv? I know she's only got a couple more weeks before she takes off. We've worked out all the details about her house. Do you feel weird about me moving in there?"

"No. Not at all, I'm glad it worked out. It—it's not Viv," she said. "I mean, I am bummed about her going so far away, but we've talked a bunch and I'm feeling better about her decision. She's definitely got her head on straighter this time. I think they both have their relationship as the priority this time."

"That's a good thing," Trevor said. "I know it must be hard when his career demands such a radical change for her, though. It's one of the reasons I never let myself get serious about anyone when I was in the service."

Christy cocked her head. "What if you'd met someone who made you want to get serious?"

He cocked his head right back, those blue eyes probing hers. "I suppose we would have had to make some tough decisions."

"Would you have left the military if it meant losing her if you didn't?"

Trevor laughed, obviously surprised by the line of questioning. "I don't know. I might have." He sobered and gently laid his hands on her shoulders. "Most of the places I went weren't fit for spouses, much less families. The risk factor was also pretty high. I never wanted to put someone in that position. So I was careful to make sure I wasn't ever tempted to."

"Was your dad in positions like that? Did you worry about him?"

"Fortunately, no. We moved often, but he was command staff pretty early on, so there was no direct risk to him. Not really."

"Yet he never remarried."

"No. He didn't." He studied her. "Where is all this coming from? What are you really worried about?"

She shook her head, not even sure herself. "I guess it's all the thinking I've done about Viv and Eric. It's made me sort of reflective about relationships. I think of Kate and Mike on their wedding day, the way they looked at each other when they came out of the chapel. Viv and Eric looked like that, too. Then it all went south so quickly." She shrugged. "I know they're working on it, but it's still sort of scary to think about. I guess I think about my mom, too. I wonder why she can't just let go of her marriage-or-bust attitude and be happy alone. It seems like such a crapshoot, to allow yourself to care like that, put yourself in a position where someone else has so much control over your feelings and emotional well-being."

Christy wasn't sure what she expected him to say. She couldn't even believe she was saying all this. Was she trying to shock him? Scare him off? She wasn't sure what she was doing. She just knew she was confused and it felt right to talk to him about it.

"Would being alone guarantee your mother happiness?" *Or you?*

He hadn't said the last part out loud, but she'd heard the question all the same. She couldn't answer for herself. A few months ago, maybe, but not any longer. "She's never really tried being alone. One relationship ends and she's on the hunt for the next one. I guess I can't imagine defining who I am by whether or not I'm with someone else."

He tipped her chin up. "And you don't. You're not your mother. You're not Viv or Kate, either. You're you. You've got your head on pretty straight, you seem to know what you want. As much as anybody can. So what is it you're really trying to say here? Do you want to stop seeing me?"

Stunned, Christy froze. "No. No, not at all. I guess I— I'm just trying to sort it all out, because—"

He grinned then. "Because why? Because when you weren't looking, you somehow ended up in a relationship that might mean something to you?" He traced those long fingers over her cheeks and across her lips, making her tremble. "You mean something to me, Christy. And if you want to know if I think this is serious, then the answer is yes, I do."

She trembled harder. God, why couldn't this be easier? Why couldn't she just throw all her hard-won caution to the wind, say what the hell and fling herself at him?

"I don't want you to give up anything of yourself for me. That's the reason I enjoy being with you— the fact that you're sure of who you are and don't need to try and be anything else. Not for me, not for anyone. I want to be with you, enjoy you. Enjoy the way you make me feel, enjoy the pleasure we share in each other's company.''

''I—I want all those things, too.''

He slid his fingers into her hair. ''Then we don't have any problems, do we?''

But even as his mouth claimed hers, and she let the thrill of him slide all throughout her body...she couldn't help but feel like she was somehow waiting for the other shoe to drop.

13

THE OTHER SHOE HIT the floor a couple of weeks later. Actually, it felt more like a whole closet of shoes.

The first shoe had actually come when Viv left for Sweden. Christy had missed her instantly. Viv had called several times and seemed very optimistic. Christy was truly happy for her, even if she selfishly wished Viv were here so she could dump all her insecurities on her.

Instead she'd done the next best thing and started pulling double shifts wherever she could. She told herself it was to pay for the renovations she still had planned, but it was really avoidance. She also knew that somewhere deep inside she was testing Trevor. Yet he'd been nothing but understanding and patient with her. Dammit.

The second shoe had been the night of the accident. She'd gotten off work at four in the morning and her only desire was to get home to bed. Instead she'd been first on scene at a nasty car accident. She'd called it in and jumped out in the pouring rain to see if she could help. Paramedics had arrived as she was performing CPR on an older man who'd been banged up pretty badly. They took over, but the old man kept calling for someone named George.

Christy was afraid there had been another person in the car with him, but if there had been, he wasn't in the car now. So she'd gone to look for George. After twenty minutes she'd finally given up. The accident victims had been transported, she'd talked to the officers on the scene and been given permission to go.

She'd headed back to her car...and found George. All one hundred and fifty soaking, filthy, slobbery pounds of him. Part Saint Bernard, part God-knew-what, he'd been happily waiting for her in the driver seat of her car. In her haste to get to the victims, she'd left the door open and George had apparently taken that as an open invitation. He hadn't spent all his time in the driver's seat, either, as the entire inside of her car was covered in splatters of mud, grit, water and...well, she shuddered to think of what else was there.

She had no idea what to do with him. The fireman and police on scene offered to transport him to the pound, but Christy couldn't bring herself to do that to him. Besides, she couldn't get him to leave her car. She decided to keep him—for one night—until she could talk to the old man when she went on shift and find out where he wanted him to stay.

As it happened, the old man didn't make it. His final request was for Christy to give the dog a good home. A dying wish the old man's lawyer was more

than willing to agree to, as there were no living rel-
atives who wanted the beast. Trevor had stepped in
and offered to take George. Kind and understanding Trevor. It had been love at first slobber for the
two of them. Trevor had always wanted a dog, but
his lifestyle, both as a child and as an adult, had pre-
cluded having one. He'd already built the dog a
huge play yard, house and whatnot at his training
compound, but that still meant George came home
with him at night. Home being, for the most part,
Christy's place.

The third shoe had dropped when Christy had
arisen three mornings ago to the sounds of banging
and cursing emanating from her downstairs bathroom. She'd stumbled down the stairs to find an old
guy named Jimmy busily ripping out her toilet and
bathroom sink. Helpful, thoughtful, Trevor had
struck again. This time with porcelain fixtures.

But all of that paled to this morning. The final
shoe had just whapped her upside the head like an
army boot. She'd been all cuddled in Trevor's very
warm, all-too-perfect arms, happy to have a day off.
So happy, in fact, she was even ignoring George's
snoring, bed-hogging presence. Jimmy wasn't due
over until later that day to start ripping out the upstairs bathroom. She had to admit he'd done a wonderful job on the downstairs and that Trevor had
found the perfect fixtures at a really good price.

Right at that moment, she was willing to admit
that maybe, just maybe, everything was going to

work out and that, in fact, life could be this disgust-ingly perfect.

She should have known better than to drop her guard, even for a second.

"Yoo-hoo!"

Christy sat bolt upright. Only one voice could wake her up better than a dozen alarm clocks. "Oh. My. God."

Trevor mumbled something and tried to pull her back down. George snorted, snuffled and rooted around with his nose, never opening his eyes. Christy, however, remained stubbornly upright, more awake than she had any right to be on her day off.

"You up there, sweetie? The hospital said it was your day off, so I thought I'd surprise you."

Oh, it's a surprise all right. Christy didn't have time to answer, much less grab clothes. The best she could do was yank the covers from under George to preserve whatever little modesty might be left to her before—

"Oh, my!"

Christy sighed. "Hi, Mom."

"What a nice surprise," Trevor offered from be-hind her.

Christy shot a look at him. He'd propped himself up on one elbow behind her, as casual and relaxed as if he were meeting Ruby Russell at a trendy res-taurant...rather than while naked in her daughter's bed.

Ruby smiled, never one to be taken aback for long.

"Why yes, this certainly is. I don't believe we've had the pleasure." She cast a long look at Christy. "You never even mentioned you had a new beau."

Trevor's brows lifted. "You didn't tell your mother about us?"

"Well, I—"

"How long have you two known each other?" Ruby asked.

"Not one word about me?"

Christy looked from her mother to Trevor, clutching the sheet to her chest. George roused his head and stared at her accusingly, too. Oh, great. Even the dog wouldn't come to her defense. "I saved your life, you know," she reminded him, to no good effect.

Her mother and Trevor began talking at the same time, George started barking at the excitement until Christy finally cut them all off with a sharp whistle. "Okay!"

Her mother's perfectly lined mouth dropped open, then snapped shut. George plopped his head down in her lap, almost yanking the sheet from her grasp. Trevor simply stared at her, patiently waiting. Perfectly patient, that was Trevor.

Well, she wasn't perfect at much of anything, most especially at being found in bed—naked and not alone—by her own mother. She shoved at the dog's head, glaring at Trevor, who was grinning now. "This is not remotely amusing." She turned to her mother, ignoring the fact that Trevor's grin hadn't faded one twitch. "Mom, if you don't mind waiting downstairs, we'll meet you down there momentarily."

George chose that moment to drag his huge body off the bed and trot over to Ruby who, to Christy's shock, patted his head, then turned and motioned the huge beast toward the stairs. "Come on, handsome. You can help me make some coffee while we let the two lovebirds get dressed."

Christy was still staring, openmouthed as they went down the stairs together.

"Your mother seemed to handle that pretty well. She seems nice enough."

Christy just glared at him. "Oh, my mother is a perfect angel. When she wants to be."

"I take it she doesn't usually like dogs."

Christy shook her head. "Dog hair and slobber don't go well with couture and diamonds, don't you know?"

"She does know how to dress," he said with the same frank male appreciation Christy had heard countless times.

"I know what you're thinking," she said. "Where did I hatch from, right?" Ruby Russell was a trim five foot two, with curves in all the right places, hair as richly colored as her name and a face that belonged to a woman at least a decade and a half younger than her sixty-two years. "I take after my dad, obviously. They were your typical peasant-meets-royalty romance. My mother being the royalty."

Trevor tugged her back down on the bed and

rolled on top of her, cutting off her squealed protest with a devastating kiss. "I think you got the best of both," he said when he finally let her up for air.

Before she could respond, he was off the bed and snatching up his clothes. "If you'd like some time with her alone, I can go for a run, take a long shower, whatever."

Christy made a face at him.

He laughed. "What was that for?"

"Tell me the truth. You're really an android or something, right? Built to be the perfect man, always knowing the right thing to say, the right thing to do, never losing his temper."

Trevor's eyes lit up and she waited for the perfect bantering response, but he must have seen something in her eyes. He even knew when to tease her and when not to. Would his perfection never end?

He sat on the side of the bed. "I'm hardly perfect."

"Seem that way to me."

"Why is it I don't think you meant that as a compliment?"

"Because you're sharp and in tune to my every mood?"

He just looked at her. "Is that why you didn't tell your mother about me? Because I'm too sharp and in tune to your every mood? What's really going on here?"

She tried to figure out how to put it into words. "We never fight."

He gaped at her. "What? And that's a bad thing?"

"It's not...normal. You're always so damned understanding. I swear I could work a million shifts in a row and you'd just be waiting here to rub my feet when I got home. It's enough to make me crazy, Trevor!"

"Okay, then. No more foot rubs." He grinned. "Unless you beg me."

She flopped back on the bed. "See? That's just what I mean. I can't even work up a good mad against you. You always charm me right out of it."

He surprised her by flipping himself fully onto the bed and on top of her, pinning her arms and legs neatly in the process. "You make me happy, Christy. You make me want to make you happy. Don't you understand? I love you."

"Yeah, well, I don't care what you— What did you just say?"

He wasn't grinning now. In fact, his face was as serious as she'd ever seen it. "I said I love you." He dropped a heartbreakingly gentle kiss on her lips. "I've only wanted to say it a million times, but I didn't want you to push me completely away."

"But—"

"I'm not stupid. I know that this whole relationship has got you scared. It should scare me, too. But it doesn't. You're everything I've ever wanted, Christy. I feel like I've known you all of my life. Maybe more than one lifetime. I don't know, I can't explain it. Even when you're grumpy, maybe especially then, I just want to hold you, touch you, love you. I can't help it. And I don't want to. It's not an act, or a game. I'm sure we'll find something we disagree on enough to lose our tempers. Probably more times than we'll be able to keep count." A smile played around his mouth. "I'm just as sure making up will be almost worth the fight." He leaned down and brushed his lips over her forehead, then the tip of her nose, then her mouth. "But I'm in this for the duration. For as long as you'll have me. And I want you to have me for a very, very long time."

He waited, but she was stunned speechless.

"Well, that's reassuring," he said finally, the tiniest bit of temper in his voice. "But you might as well get used to it. I love you, Christy Russell." He kissed her then, hard and fast, almost angry.

It shouldn't have turned her on. But it did. Almost more than his declaration of love and commitment.

She was still clambering for something to say when he abruptly climbed off of her. He looked angry, which made no sense since he'd just told her he loved her. *Now* he loses his cool?

"What I don't want is you questioning what we have together," he said tersely. "You need to make up your mind. Do you want us enough to work for it? Or don't you? I'm not asking for a lifetime commitment right this second, though you should know I'd take it in a heartbeat. I just want to know if this is important enough to you to give it a shot. If *I'm* important to you." He turned toward the bathroom. "Let's start with that."

"Wait." She finally found her voice, but she still didn't know what to say. This whole thing had taken her by surprise. Maybe it shouldn't have; she'd been pushing him hard enough. But she was stunned nevertheless. She needed time. She needed Viv. She needed a drink...or whatever the equivalent was at nine in the morning. "Where are you—"

"I'm going for a run," he said, cutting her off. "A long one." Without looking at her, he closed the bathroom door behind him.

Christy stared at the door and felt the first stirrings of panic. It was only a piece of wood, but he'd never purposely shut her out before. It might as well have been a solid foot of concrete. Suddenly the idea of pushing him didn't seem so wise. She didn't want to lose him. She'd just wanted things to stay simple, not get all complicated.

Well, he'd gone and changed that now. She didn't know if she wanted to dance on her mattress...or throw something at the door. How dare he put it all in her lap?

She dragged herself out of bed, pulling on sweats and a T-shirt and not bothering to comb her hair. She grabbed her socks, then sunk back down on the edge of the bed as it hit her all over again. He loved her. Really and truly. Talk about a shoe dropping!

She realized she hadn't given him the words back. She looked at the door he'd closed between them.

"Honey, where's the sweetener?"

Christy groaned. Trevor had done the impossible. He'd made her forget about her mother. "In the blue-covered dish by the fridge," she yelled down the stairs. This was the worst possible time for Trevor to have dropped this bomb on her. She needed to think. She needed to place an emergency call to Sweden. She needed...time.

She darted a look at the door and realized she wasn't ready to face him again, so she quickly went downstairs to unashamedly hide behind her mother. After all, if she was going to have to suffer the conversation she knew was in the offing, the least her mother could do in return was provide a decent demilitarized zone.

She'd just stepped into the kitchen when Trevor jogged down the stairs and paused by the kitchen door. He was wearing ancient navy-blue sweats and a T-shirt with the sleeves torn out. She'd look like a bag lady in that getup. Trevor, on the other hand, looked totally studly.

"It was a pleasure meeting you, ma'am," he said.

"Ruby, please," her mother replied, all smiles. She obviously appreciated Trevor's military manners...and his fashion sense, as well.

"Ruby," Trevor said, with a nod. "We're both off tonight if you'd like to join us for dinner. I don't know what your tastes are, but we can whip up something."

Ruby looked to Christy in obvious delight at the invite. Christy pasted on a smile. Apparently Trevor was going to try some pushing of his own. Well, she wasn't sure she'd bear up under it with the same graciousness and understanding he had.

"You have a date," Ruby told Trevor. "I look forward to getting to know you better."

Trevor didn't even look at Christy. "So do I, Ruby. So do I." Then he was gone.

Her mother leaned dramatically against the counter and fanned her face. "Well, my dear, you might be a late bloomer, but how clever of you to wait so you could snag the gardener himself."

"*Mom.*"

Ruby waved her complaining tone away. "Oh, don't Mom me. If anyone is an expert about these things, it's me." She poured them both a mug of coffee then perched on one of the woven wicker chairs in the nook area. She patted the one next to her. "Come on, sit. Fill me in."

Christy clasped her mug in both hands, but stayed where she was. She really needed to talk about the whole new turn her relationship with Trevor had taken. But her mother was the last person she wanted to have that talk with. Instead, she said, "What brings you to town?" Ruby loved nothing more than to talk about her latest adventures. For once, Christy was dying to hear about them. Anything to get the focus off of her and Trevor.

Ruby wagged a perfectly manicured finger at her. "Don't think you're getting away with this. I'm not leaving here until I hear all the juicy details. But since you asked, I did come here to tell you something."

"You're getting married again."

Ruby didn't look offended by her less-than-enthusiastic tone. "Nope, not this time."

Christy frowned. "You're not sick, are you?" For all that she and her mother had never had the most traditional relationship, Christy loved her mother unconditionally. She reached out and placed her hand on her mother's shoulder. "Tell me what's wrong." She sank down in the opposite chair.

"Oh, sweetie, I'm sorry, I didn't mean to worry you," Ruby said with a smile. "Although I'm glad to see you'd worry about me if something was wrong. I guess I did something right with you after all."

"Of course I'd worry about you," Christy said, then with a dry smile, she added, "and I'm a perfectly wonderful person, so you must have done everything right."

"Yes, you are perfectly wonderful, but you deserve as much credit as I do, if not more, for turning out that way."

"Thank you, but I'm hardly feeling wonderful at the moment," she murmured as she sipped her coffee, then wished the words back when the gleam came into her mother's eyes.

"Looks like things are pretty serious with you and the hunk if he's comfortable enough inviting me to have dinner at your place. And I take it he cooks, too, since we both know I failed you horribly when it came to teaching you to make anything more than reservations. Although I suppose I could be coerced into learning to chop vegetables if it meant being near someone who looks like him. So, when did he move in?"

Christy's head was already beginning to throb. "We're just dating. He—"

Ruby snorted. "Remember who you're talking to. I saw the way he looked at you. I also happened to notice he was perfectly at ease in your bed." She wagged a finger. "And while you may not tell me everything—"

"Gee, I wonder why?"

Ruby continued, unfazed as always by sarcasm. "I do know that you don't jump into bed with anyone you're not really serious about. So you might as well just tell me. I know I can be...well, traditional about some things."

Christy almost snorted coffee through her nose. "Traditional?"

"I certainly am not one to—how does your generation put it? Shack up? You know how I feel about marriage." She eyed Christy closely, as if expecting a comeback, but Christy managed to look completely innocent.

Ruby sighed. "Dear, I know I'm old-fashioned about some things. But I'm certainly hip enough to understand if you're living together. Of course, I'll want you to marry the man. And really, he is a total—"

"He has his own place, Mom," Christy cut in. "Well, he's actually staying at Viv's house, but—"

"He's living with Vivian, too?" Ruby said, stunned. "I can't believe you'd put up with—"

"Mom, please! Viv is in Sweden. With Eric. Trevor is just subletting her place while she's gone. And we're just dating." She wasn't sure who she was trying to convince more with that last part.

"So Vivian finally wised up, did she?"

Christy's mouth dropped open. "Wised up? I hardly think that—"

"Actually, hardly thinking is usually better in these sorts of circumstances, dear. Instinct, that's what should rule. It's good she finally listened to her heart. Come now, don't look so shocked. You've always known those two were meant for one another."

"But Eric—"

"Wanted his career and he wanted his wife to support his choices. Men are like that. But trust me, sweetie, she could have had anything she wanted if she'd played her cards right. I was at the wedding, remember? I saw how he looked at her." She looked at her daughter and Christy knew where she was headed with that train of thought.

"What about Viv's career? Her choices?" Christy held up her hand. "Never mind. I don't want to have this discussion, okay?"

"Well, I do. You might be surprised, given my history with men. But why is it, do you think, that I am usually the one who breaks things off? Hmm? Because I stand up for myself, that's why. And a lot of men my age...and a few that aren't," she added with a grin, "can't accept that. All of which means that they weren't right for me." She leaned forward.

"Tell me this. Did she go running off to Eric...or did he come back here for her?"

"He came back here, but—"

"Exactly. They both have wants, both have aspirations, but ultimately, what is most important is that they have each other. They realize this now and they'll work for it."

"Still—"

Ruby just smiled. "Honey, I'm here to tell you, when you find the man that is your true mate, the one you can't stand to be without, well then, the rungs on the priority ladder get all rearranged. Careers are satisfying, yes, but growing old with someone who loves you? Who wants to share your good days and your bad? Who wants to raise a family with you? Careers sort of pale in comparison to that."

Christy sat back, stunned by the passion she heard in her mother's voice. "But—"

"Your father was that to me," she said quietly. "And I've never found another like him." Ruby stared into her mug. "Maybe I've been afraid, too. Watching the man you love more than anything slowly die in front of your eyes..." She shuddered and Christy covered her hand.

"You never told me," she said, awed and humbled by the love her mother and father must have shared.

"You had your own grief to deal with. And, I admit, I dealt with mine in my own way. Alone." Ruby looked up with tears in her beautiful eyes. "I never wanted to risk that kind of pain again. Maybe that's why I married men I knew couldn't stand up to me for long." She tried to smile. "You know, all the fun without the risk. But that's not enough. Not for me. And it shouldn't be for you." Her lips trembled and she gripped her daughter's hand with surprising strength. "It's not fun growing old alone, Christy. Nor is it fun to make do. And I won't make do, not any longer. Maybe it's too late, I don't know. Maybe Mr. Right has already passed me by. But I'm not willing to put up with Mr. Okay-For-Now anymore."

Christy didn't know what to say. For the second time this morning she'd been left speechless by a passionate declaration from a person she loved.

"I came back to Richmond because I want to be with you. You're my family and you're what's most important. I want to build a life here that includes you. If I get lucky in love, so be it. But I do know I love you best, so here is where I want to be. I hope that's okay with you."

Christy launched out of her seat and pulled her mother into a tight hug, tears swimming in her eyes. "Of course it's okay. I love you best, too."

She also realized something else. She thought her mother wouldn't understand what she was going through, when in fact, her mother was probably the perfect person to talk to. "I—I need to talk to you. About Trevor."

Fresh tears sprang to her mother's eyes. "I thought you'd never ask."

"He—" Christy swallowed. "He told me he loves me."

"Darling, that's wonderful!"

Christy smiled, for the first time letting herself really believe it. "Yes," she said, almost in awe of the power of it. "Yes, it is."

"So, what's the problem? He's gorgeous, he cooks, he obviously worships the ground you walk on. It looks like you're already setting up house together, no matter what you say." She looked down to where George was lying in a huge sprawl at their feet. "You've even started a family."

Christy eyed George dolefully, but decided not to respond to that. "It's all happening so fast."

"Is he pressuring you to marry him? Or something else you're not comfortable with?"

"No, no, that's not it. He only told me he loved me just this morning."

Ruby clapped her hands in delight, then looked dismayed. "Oh, and then I came barging in. Oh, dear. I'm so sorry!"

"No, no. He told me after you barged in," Christy said, smiling. Then her smile faded. "He was sort of...angry when he said it. I guess I've been... well..."

"Playing hard to get? Oh my, dear. If he's the right one, you should never play games."

"I wasn't playing games," Christy said, indignant. "I just... It just seemed like it was moving so fast. I mean—one minute he's dragging me out of

Viv's bed and the next thing I know we're practically living together."

"I'll want to hear more about that first part. But let me ask you something. Just what is the appropriate amount of time falling in love should take?"

"I—" Christy closed her mouth. She had no idea. She'd never really thought about it that way.

Her mother covered her hand again, and this time Christy drew strength from it. "Do you love him?"

Christy took a deep breath, then let it out again. "When you talked about growing old together, spending good days and bad...I realized I can't imagine that with anyone else but him." She smiled, feeling both panicky and joyous. "That must be love, right?"

Her mother beamed. "Sounds like it to me."

"But it's all so scary," Christy said, almost to herself.

"Yes, dear, it is." Her mother smiled knowingly. "But trust me, it's the best kind of scary in the world."

"That's basically what Viv told me," she said shakily.

Her mother took her hand again, but this time Christy felt something entirely new. Real understanding, and trust.

"You should listen to her. And me. But most of all, listen to your heart."

Christy nodded. "Now I just have to convince

him I really do know what I want. I haven't exactly inspired confidence in that area lately."

Her mother beamed, patted her hand and pulled them both up to a stand. "Well, you've come to the right place."

14

TREVOR WASN'T SURE what to expect when he arrived back at Christy's place. In fact, he thought about avoiding it altogether and going over to the compound to get some work done. He told himself it was to let Christy and her mom have more time, but he knew better. He was afraid. Afraid he'd pushed too hard, too fast. Which was why he continued to head for the condo. No way was he going to let her run from this.

So maybe he shouldn't have pushed it this particular morning. Of all the moments to finally tell her he loved her, the morning her mother shows up was probably not the best one. He'd run ten miles and her stunned reaction was still etched in his memory. He could probably run a marathon and still see that expression clearly in his mind.

He'd been so patient, fully prepared to take as long as necessary to convince her that this was the real thing. What would she do now that he'd pushed her to make a decision? Would she back away from the relationship? Tell him she needed her space, or something equally frustrating? He stopped and braced his hands on his knees, sweat running freely down his face now. Why in the hell had he pushed her? Things had been going great between them. If he'd just waited.... He stretched and continued walking. But dammit, he loved her! And he wanted the freedom of being able to tell her so whenever he felt like it, which, lately had been at least a hundred times a day.

And, honestly, he was dying to hear those words from her lips. Sure, he loved her confidence and her certainty about things, just as he loved her vulnerabilities, including her hang-ups about relationships. The very fact that she'd welcomed him into her home, into her bed, told him he was special to her. But he wanted more. He wanted the words. It shocked him how badly he needed the words.

He stopped at the door to the stairwell that led to her condo. *So, what's the strategy now, McQuillen?*

The words had been said, he couldn't take them back. And, he realized now, he didn't want to. Maybe this was the only way they were going to push their relationship to the next level. She knew by now she could trust him. And she had to know how she felt about him. He simply wasn't going to let her hide in her safety zone any longer.

And what if she tells you she can't handle anything more? That stopped him, but only for a second. He opened the door and sprinted up the stairs. Then so be it, he thought. But she was going to have to give him some pretty damn good reasons why.

He was praying her mother was gone, because he'd worked himself up for this big confrontation and he really didn't want to play host at the moment. One way or the other, they were going to have this out. Now. Today.

Just as he reached for the knob, the door swung open and Ruby stepped out. "Oh, my!" she said, but didn't really seem all that put off at finding him standing there all hot and sweaty.

"Sorry to startle you, ma'am."

Ruby beamed up at him. "My, that's nice. I've always loved military manners."

Trevor found himself grinning, despite the pile of emotions that were squirming inside him. "Yes, ma'am."

"I was just on my way out." She tugged on the leash he now noticed she had in her hand. "Come on, big boy."

"Are you taking him for a walk?" Trevor asked in obvious surprise as George bustled out the door behind her. "Because I've been working with him, but he still gets excited when he sees people or other animals. He's very strong and—"

Ruby patted Trevor on the cheek as he reached down to pet George's huge head. He didn't think he'd ever been patted on the cheek before.

"Not to worry," Ruby said, and Trevor realized where Christy got her confidence from. "I can handle him."

Trevor straightened and gave her a sharp salute. "Why, I believe you can, ma'am."

Ruby tossed him a saucy salute of her own and

headed down the hallway toward the stairs, George trotting happily beside her.

It didn't occur to Trevor until he stepped into the condo that Ruby had her purse and keys with her when she left. Just what was going on? But that question and any others he might have had vanished the moment he stepped past the small foyer into the living room.

The curtains had been drawn against the morning sun. Instead, the room was filled with the soft, flickering light of dozens of candles. Trevor wasn't aware Christy liked candles, much less had so many of them tucked away. It gave him pause, the realization that there was still a lot he didn't know about her. But the pause was a short one. Because he knew, without doubt, that he wanted to continue being surprised by her for a lifetime.

Now if he could just find her amongst all the shadows and...what were all those pillows doing in the middle of the floor? "Christy?"

He heard a muffled response coming from somewhere up in the loft. He headed that way. "Christy?"

"Don't come up," she called out, just as his hand hit the railing.

He stopped. "Okay."

"Why don't you take a shower?" she suggested. "I'm uh—just go shower, okay?"

She sounded almost...panicked. Trevor bit back a smile. What had she cooked up here? "Okay. Can you toss me down some fresh clothes?"

"Can you just go get in the shower? Please?" She sounded exasperated.

"Yes, ma'am. Anything you say, ma'am."

He thought he heard her mutter something that sounded like "smartass" but he couldn't be sure. Well, whatever was going on, he would let her handle it her own way. But he planned on taking the quickest shower known to man.

He'd barely lathered up when there was a pounding on the door. "You almost done?"

Anxious, he decided. She sounded both anxious and exasperated. Panic was still there, too. He could only hope this was a good sign. Christy never panicked about anything unless it moved her out of her comfort zone. Their relationship had definitely put a crimp in that area. But that still didn't explain what—

"Trevor?"

"I'm coming," he said, rinsing off quickly and shutting off the water. He dried off, then wrapped the towel around his waist for lack of anything else to put on.

She was already opening the door before he could turn the handle. "Close your eyes," she instructed before flipping off the light switch.

He did as she asked. "What's going on here?"

"You're being kidnapped."

"What?"

"Just hush and bend down a little so I can tie this around your eyes."

"You want me to help you abduct me?"

"Trevor."

He smiled in the dark and bent his knees so she could reach his head. "Do I get to put some clothes on?"

"I don't recall being given that same opportunity."

Trevor stilled then. So this was payback? Well, he was game. In fact, his senses were on full alert...the result of which was arousing rather than alarming. "Can I ask where you're taking me?"

She fumbled with the fabric but finally got it tied at the back of his head. "Not far. I guess you could call this more of a hostage situation."

He straightened, fully aware that he was mostly naked, standing in the dark, blindfolded...and growing harder by the second. "Hostage, huh?" he said, hearing the hoarseness in his voice.

Her hands were on him then, turning him around. She pulled his arms in front of him and quickly tied them together at the wrist. It shouldn't have been that exciting. In fact, he was certain he wouldn't have enjoyed this kind of thing at all. *Tell that to your body.*

She grabbed his bound wrists and tugged him from the steamy bathroom. When the cooler air brushed his skin, it only sensitized him further. He could smell the candles, feel the thick carpet beneath his toes.

"Stop here," she said, then he felt her step in front of him before he was gently tugged forward again.

"Careful," she instructed. "There are pillows on the floor."

They went a few steps, then she stopped him again. "Okay, kneel."

"I beg your pardon?"

She tugged on his wrists. "Just do it, okay?"

He shook his head, but did as she asked, his knees landing on a huge, soft pillow. He wondered if she could see how aroused he was. He wondered what she'd do next. She didn't seem as turned on by the situation as he was. She was nervous. "What next?"

"Just stay there. I'll be right back."

The first little prickles of alarm crept along his neck. Had he made her so upset earlier that she'd cooked up some scheme to— No, no, she wouldn't do that. "Christy?"

Suddenly her mouth was right next to his ear, and he felt the warmth of her body behind him. "Do you trust me, Trevor?"

"Absolutely." And he realized he did and immediately relaxed. Well, part of him relaxed.

He felt her sigh against the skin of his neck. "Good, that's good." Then there was a rustle of fabric and he felt her move away from him.

She was only gone for a minute. He heard the clink of glassware, then the rustle of fabric again. The pillows shifted around his knees and he knew she was right in front of him.

"Okay," she said, more to herself than to him. "Ready."

"Christy—"

"Shh. I'm trying to do something here. Let me finish."

He bowed and smiled. "Are we going to do it all blindfolded and bound up? Because I have to tell you, I didn't think I would like this kind of thing...but you might have hit on something here."

"What?"

She didn't sound seductive, she sounded... distracted.

"Nothing. Just...do with me what you will."

"If you'll just give me a minute." She sounded like she was under some sort of strain. Then there was a popping sound, followed by a squeal and the splash of something cold on his knees. He sucked in his breath, but the whole thing only served to heighten his arousal. Whatever she was trying to do, obviously it meant a great deal to her, so he'd play along. But he'd also decided that at some point this was going to end with him buried deep inside her. They could figure out the rest later.

"Okay," she said, almost breathlessly. "You can take off the blindfold now."

"Um, I can't. My hands."

"Oh! Right, right. I forgot. I only did that so you wouldn't try to...you know, distract me." She still sounded nervous, only now he heard the smile, too.

There was another clinking of glasses then he felt her fingertips brushing against the skin of his wrists. He couldn't help it. He moaned. Just a little, but it made her pause. "Christy—" His voice was definitely rough this time.

"Pull off the blindfold," she said, her voice shaky.

He did, but rather than a sea of pillows and endless rows of lit candles, the only thing he saw was her. She kneeled just in front of him, wrapped in something sheer and incredibly sexy. She wasn't one for frilly lingerie, so this was a definite surprise. "You look amazing," he said.

"I, uh, thanks." She ran a hand over her hair, which still looked as tousled and sexy as it did when she woke up this morning. Her eyes went wide. "My hair! Dammit, I forgot all about— I knew I wasn't cut out for—"

"You're beautiful, Christy." He'd never meant anything more in his life. "And it has nothing to do with the bit of nothing you're wearing or the wild curls around your face, though I love them both."

She smiled then, still self-conscious but equally determined to brazen it out. He realized what she was doing. She was trying to show him she loved him.

"You didn't have to go to all this trouble, you know," he said quietly.

She made a face. "Try telling my mother that."

Trevor laughed. "This was Ruby's idea?"

"Just the pillows, candles and this." She fingered the sheer robe she had on. "It only took her thirty minutes to round all this stuff up." She looked at him and he saw she was trembling. "She thinks momentous occasions deserve equally momentous settings."

Trevor realized he was trembling a little now,

also. "What is the momentous occasion?" *Just tell me, Christy,* he begged silently, suddenly dying to hear her say the words.

Instead she picked up a wineglass and handed it to him, then picked the other one up for herself. "I—I want to propose. A—a toast."

"Okay." He didn't bother telling her it was only ten in the morning.

"To Trevor," she began. The champagne in the glass vibrated as her hand shook. He longed to cover it with his own, but he could see by the steely look in her eyes that it was important to her to get through this on her own. He didn't think he could love her more, but in that moment he realized he'd probably love her more every day.

"You—you came into my life by—by accident." She took a quick sip, then laughed. "Bubbles. Tickle." She quickly cleared her throat and started again. "Okay, okay," she coached herself. She took a deep breath and looked him in the eye. "From the moment you literally swept me off my feet, my life has never been the same. You've been kind, patient, loving and more understanding than I deserved."

He opened his mouth, but she shushed him.

"Let me get through this. It's important."

He nodded, because he knew it was.

"I know I haven't always been kind, or patient, or understanding in return, although you deserved it more than anyone. I—I guess I was scared. Scared of all the things I was feeling, of all the things you made me want. I've always been determined to never need anyone...like that. It's just been recently that I've started to figure out that maybe total independence is not always such a good thing. That maybe, with the right person, I can be both independent...and dependent." She sniffled, then took another fortifying sip of champagne. "What I'm trying to say is, I need you. I'm dependent on you to be there for me when I've had a rough shift. I want you there to share things with, to watch the days go by with, to...to hold me when it thunders outside." She took another breath...and another sip. "And—and I want to be there for you like that. I do think you're worth fighting for and if you'll forgive me for being too stupid to believe in what was staring me right in the face, I promise to do whatever it takes to keep us happy and together." She ran out of words and breath at the same time. She sipped her champagne again and seemed to waver on her knees as she stared at him expectantly.

Trevor was wavering a bit, too, but it had nothing to do with champagne as he hadn't tasted so much as a drop. He set his glass down and took hers as well, then reached for her hands. He rubbed at her cold fingers as he looked into the eyes that he'd come to love so deeply, it should have shocked him. But didn't. "There's just one thing I need."

"Which is?"

"Three words. From you. In fact, I've never needed to hear anything as badly as I need to hear them."

Her eyes widened as she realized what he was

asking for. "I can't believe I didn't say them!" She shut her eyes. "I knew I'd screw this up."

Trevor laughed and pulled her fully into his arms. "You didn't screw anything up. And I'm prepared to offer you a deal."

He rolled her to her back, delighting in the way the gossamer robe she wore fell open. His towel had disappeared somewhere, as well.

"What deal?" she asked, then gasped as he settled himself between her legs.

"You have to promise to say them every single day for the rest of your life."

She relaxed beneath him then, finally, her saucy smile returning. "Oh, what a hard bargain you drive."

"You don't know the half of it," he groaned, pushing against her.

She gasped as he nudged just inside her.

"If it makes it easier, I can go first," he said.

She shook her head. "No. Me first." She framed his face with her hands. "I have never felt about anyone the way I feel about you. It overwhelms me how much I need you. But what makes it all okay is knowing that you love me. I love you, Trevor Mc-Quillen. I love you."

He pushed inside her then, hard and fast, thrilled to find her wet and ready for him. "I love you, Christy," he said as she met him, thrust for thrust.

It didn't take long for them to reach the peak and go roaring right over it.

They were both still panting when Christy swore.

Trevor rolled them to their sides. "Are you okay? Did I hurt you?"

"Oh, I'm fine. It's just...Mom will be so disappointed, but I was so nervous I forgot to tell you about the roses."

"Roses?"

"Petals, actually. While she was doing the candles I was plucking rose petals and putting them on our bed. She said it's really romantic to make love in flower petals and I completely forgot."

Trevor grinned and reached down to take a nipple in his mouth, delighting in her gasp of pleasure. "Gee, I can't imagine what distracted you."

"I knew I should never have untied your hands."

"But then, I couldn't do this." He slid his hand down between her legs, making her gasp again and buck her hips.

"True," she said a bit breathlessly. "Absolutely true."

"And there's no reason we can't go play in the petals now."

"You're absolutely right." She playfully nipped at his shoulder. "Did I mention I love you?"

He stilled then, still not used to the power of those words coming from her lips. "It's amazing."

"What is?"

"How incredible it makes me feel to hear you say that."

She smiled even as her eyes went a bit glassy. "Well, I'll remember that when I want to win our next argument."

"You do that. Now, about those rose petals..." He stood and offered her a hand, but when he went to pull her up, he kept pulling until she was over his shoulder.

"Trevor!" she squealed.

"I seem to recall enjoying this view of your legs once before." He climbed the stairs. "If you don't stop squirming we can always see how you like being tied up."

She stopped squirming...but only for a second.

"Oh!" he laughed, only a little shocked. "So that's how you want to play." He tossed her on the bed and pinned her down beneath him. Both of them were laughing and out of breath. "Never a dull moment with you, you know that?"

"I was thinking the same thing about you."

Just then there was a banging on the front door, then cursing as someone was letting themself in. "Can't see a blasted thing in here. What, did the power go out or something? What's with all the candles?"

Christy and Trevor both froze. "Oh, no. I forgot about Jimmy," she said a moment later.

"Power works fine," Trevor called out.

There was a pause, then, "Oh."

Christy tried not to snicker, but Trevor made a face at her and she lost it. She had to bury her face in the pillows as she roared with laughter.

"Want me to put them out before you burn the place down?"

"Would you please?" Trevor called out, ever so politely.

"No problem. I'll get to work down here then, if that's okay."

"Okay," Trevor called out, then gulped as Christy found her way under the covers and started doing wicked things with rose petals.

"Just, uh, don't plan on any showers anytime soon," Jimmy shouted. "I have to turn the water off."

"No problem," Trevor gasped.

Christy peeked out from beneath the covers. "Never a dull moment. Isn't that what you said?"

"Yeah...I believe so. Oh, God, that feels good."

But before she could go any further, an unmistakable woof filled the air.

"George," they both said at the same time. Seconds later they both oophed as he joined them enthusiastically on the bed.

"I'm so sorry, sweetie," her mom called out, sounding out of breath. "I put the convertible top down thinking he'd like the air and he just jumped right out at the light. I had to chase him all the way back here in the car."

"Who are you?" Jimmy barked.

"Oh, my!" Ruby gasped.

Christy rolled her eyes. "Jimmy and my mom. Now that should be interesting. Did I mention she was moving here?"

"Definitely no dull moments."

"I can't imagine why I ever thought it was better to live alone," she murmured dryly.

Trevor pulled her closer. "Me, either."

"I love you," she said, then squealed when George gave them both a big kiss.

"I think he's given us his slobber of approval."

Christy laughed. "He's just making sure he gets his share of the bed."

Trevor pulled her on top of him. "There, now he has more room." He pushed against her. "And I have more you."

"Trevor, my mother is downstairs."

"Keeping Jimmy entertained."

"Well...I suppose no one would mind if we—" She gasped, then moaned very softly. "I do love you, Trevor McQuillen."

It was right about then that George started sneezing.

"Oh, for God's sake," Christy sputtered.

"You think he's allergic to roses?"

"Honey, where do you want me to store all these candles?"

"Hey, Trev, ya got another extension cord?"

The phone rang.

"Honey, it's Viv!"

Trevor yanked the covers over both their heads, blocking out as much of the world as he could. "Christy, will you marry me?"

"You're proposing now?"

"I figure if you say yes in the middle of all this, I know you really want me."

She smiled. "I want you."

He kissed her, long and deeply. "We should ask Viv if we can borrow the cabin for our honeymoon."

"We might never come back."

George started sneezing again.

"That idea did occur to me."

Christy laughed and Trevor kissed her again, wondering how she felt about adding kids to the melee that was their life. Well, he probably shouldn't mention it now. But he could be patient.

"I love you," she whispered against his mouth.

Oh, yes. Very patient, indeed.

COOPER'S CORNER

In April 2002 you are invited to three wonderful weddings in a very special town...

A Wedding at Cooper's Corner

USA Today bestselling author

Kristine Rolofson
Muriel Jensen
Bobby Hutchinson

Ailing Warren Cooper has asked private investigator David Solomon to deliver three precious envelopes to each of his grandchildren. Inside each is something that will bring surprise, betrayal...and unexpected romance!

And look for the exciting launch of *Cooper's Corner*, a NEW 12-book continuity from Harlequin— launching in August 2002.

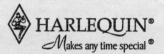

HARLEQUIN®
Makes any time special ®

Visit us at www.eHarlequin.com

PHWCC

If you enjoyed what you just read,
then we've got an offer you can't resist!

Take 2 bestselling
love stories FREE!

Plus get a FREE surprise gift!

Clip this page and mail it to Harlequin Reader Service®

IN U.S.A.	IN CANADA
3010 Walden Ave.	P.O. Box 609
P.O. Box 1867	Fort Erie, Ontario
Buffalo, N.Y. 14240-1867	L2A 5X3

YES! Please send me 2 free Harlequin Temptation® novels and my free surprise gift. After receiving them, if I don't wish to receive anymore, I can return the shipping statement marked cancel. If I don't cancel, I will receive 4 brand-new novels each month, before they're available in stores. In the U.S.A., bill me at the bargain price of $3.34 plus 25¢ shipping and handling per book and applicable sales tax, if any*. In Canada, bill me at the bargain price of $3.80 plus 25¢ shipping and handling per book and applicable taxes**. That's the complete price and a savings of 10% off the cover prices—what a great deal! I understand that accepting the 2 free books and gift places me under no obligation ever to buy any books. I can always return a shipment and cancel at any time. Even if I never buy another book from Harlequin, the 2 free books and gift are mine to keep forever.

142 HEN DFND
342 HEN DFNE

Name	(PLEASE PRINT)	
Address	Apt.#	
City	State/Prov.	Zip/Postal Code

* Terms and prices subject to change without notice. Sales tax applicable in N.Y.
** Canadian residents will be charged applicable provincial taxes and GST.
   All orders subject to approval. Offer limited to one per household and not valid to
   current Harlequin Temptation® subscribers.
   ® are registered trademarks of Harlequin Enterprises Limited.

TEMP01 ©1998 Harlequin Enterprises Limited

Back by popular request...
those amazing Buckhorn Brothers!

Once
and Again

Containing two full-length novels by
the Queen of Sizzle,

USA Today bestselling author

LORI
FOSTER

They're all gorgeous, all sexy and all single...at least for now!
This special volume brings you the sassy and seductive
stories of Sawyer and Morgan Buckhorn—offering you
hours of *hot, hot* reading!

Available in June 2002 wherever books are sold.

And in September 2002 look for FOREVER AND ALWAYS,
containing the stories of Gabe and Jordan Buckhorn!

HARLEQUIN®
Makes any time special ®

PHLF-1R